Steel Tree

Sarena Ulibarri

Android Press

Published by Android Press
Eugene, Oregon
www.android-press.com

First Printing, 2023
ISBN: 978-1958121641

Contents

THE WINTER PARTY

The Silber House felt so empty ever since Klara's parents ascended the space elevator for Petipa Colony—so empty and so in need of a party. Klara rearranged the Pirlipat tarts on their tray for the third time, snagged a stray strand of tinsel from the floor, and shined the nog pitcher with the sleeve of her velvet dress. Everything was perfect. Everything *needed* to be perfect. No one had expected her to host the annual Winter Party by herself, to keep her parents' tradition alive now that they'd left Eta. But she'd done it, and it was going to be wonderful.

Klara waited in the foyer for her guests to arrive, tapping her foot on the tile floor. Should she turn down the geothermal pump? Would the house get too warm once all those bodies packed in here? Or would the cold breeze that entered along with each guest make the house too cold? Klara couldn't remember how her parents handled such mundane details.

The light that slanted into the solarium was already tinged with the orange of sunset. Klara did another round, double- or triple-checking everything. They *would* come, wouldn't they? Did everyone have enough time to sew or print fancy new costumes for the party after they finished the winter harvest? *She'd* sewn her own red and green velvet dress, and that was after processing all the nuts for half a dozen neighboring orchards, plus her own, and with faulty nutcracker androids, at that.

Yes, she told herself. *They'll come.*

Life on the fertile moon of Eta was such a slog, growing crops to be delivered to the ships that docked at the space elevator once per season. Everyone worked their fingers to the bone with the hope that someday they'd earn their way off this simple world and join Petipa Colony on a proper planet. The Silber's Winter Party was always a bright spot during the darkest part of the year. They'd come.

The doorbell rang, and Klara danced in place before she raced over to answer it. She took a deep breath to compose herself, then put in place her practiced smile, and opened the door wide.

She'd been hoping to welcome a big group, but Louise stood there by herself, wearing a yellow flapper dress, complete with fringe and flowered headband. Klara stepped aside and waved her in, clandestinely glancing behind Louise to see if anyone else was coming.

Louise raised an eyebrow as she surveyed the foyer's decorations. "Ah, I see you went with a Christmas theme this year."

Klara shut the door. "I hope that's okay," she said, suddenly self-conscious of the silly reindeer and elves and gingerbread men.

Louise handed over her sequined jacket. "It's your party, love."

Klara's heart dropped. *She hates it. They're all going to hate it.* The doorbell rang again just as she slipped Louise's coat onto a hanger in the foyer closet.

"Ooh, Christmas!" Alicia exclaimed as soon as Klara opened the door. "I loved Christmas; we always had the best ones with my family back on Earth."

Louise rolled her eyes. "Uhg, I always found the season dreadful."

"No!" Alicia protested. She shrugged out of her white faux-fur coat and handed it to Klara. "Christmas was magical. Ice skating and cookies and everyone singing carols around the fireplace and—oh! Klara, this is the best."

"I'm glad *you* have such wonderful memories," Louise said. "What I remember about Christmas season is a lot of greed and stress. Everyone crowding shops to spend money they didn't have and fight over some bauble they wouldn't even remember the next year."

Alicia wasn't even listening. She sang, "It's the *most* wonderful time..." and waltzed around the foyer with an invisible partner.

Klara shut the coat closet, chewing her lip. "I didn't realize it would be so divisive."

"It's fine, love," Louise said. "Just comes with some baggage for us Earth babies."

"Yes, I understand," Klara said, though she really didn't. She was an Eta baby, born here a few years after her parents left Earth. They'd earned their invitation to Petipa Colony last season, but Klara hadn't been included. Eta was populated by those who couldn't afford the interstellar passage from Earth to Petipa; they tended the crops Petipa Colony depended on until the government considered their debt paid. The terms for children of debtors had always been unclear. But Klara figured if she kept doing everything exactly the way they did, she'd earn her place too.

"Well," she said as she guided Louise and Alicia into the solarium. "There are more Christmas decorations in there, for better or for worse."

Lots of them, in fact. Ice sculptures and spiral topiaries wrapped in silver tinsel. Trays of snowman-shaped cookies and peppermint cupcakes. Mistletoe draped around doorways, sparkling paper snowflakes dangled from the hanging planters. Alicia gasped when she saw the decorations, and Klara tried to conceal her delight at the reaction.

She pointed toward the curtain covering the south-facing windows. "There's a surprise for later, so no peeking!" The doorbell chimed. Klara hopped in excitement and rushed back to the foyer to greet the next set of guests.

They arrived, wearing reds and greens and golds. The women had braided beads and winter flowers into their hair, and painted elaborate designs around their eyes. The men wore embroidered robes and colorful tunics, stylish vests and festive kilts. Each of the children resembled a beautiful little doll. Klara had worried for nothing; they showed up, and every one of them looked amazing.

But then Ginger arrived, and Klara's face fell. She wore the exact same orange maxi dress she'd worn at last year's party. Her hair was a jumbled mess, and eye liner streaked across her left temple. Her half-dozen children swarmed in behind her, dressed in mismatched pieces of previous years' costumes. *No effort at all*, Klara huffed. The entire family looked like they'd gotten ready in a careless rush. She tucked her judgments away and plastered a smile back onto her face.

"I'm so sorry we're late," Ginger said.

"You're not late! But, Ginger—" Klara lowered her voice and guided the other woman away from the doorway. "Is everything okay?"

"Benjamin's still missing." She burst into tears. Horrified, Klara steered her toward the coat closet where fewer people might see the outburst. "Sorry." Ginger reached up to wipe at her eyes, transforming the single streak of eyeliner into a spiderweb. She sucked in a noisy breath and closed her eyes. "He's been gone two days."

Klara had heard about several men who were missing. She hadn't given much thought to it, because she'd been busy with the harvest and the party preparations, and also because people *didn't* just disappear on Eta. The habitable region of this moon was so small, and impassable mountains of volcanic glass surrounded their fertile valley.

"Oh, Ginger! I'm sure he'll turn up soon. I can't imagine where he's gone."

She could, though. What she imagined was that he must be sleeping off a binger in someone else's barn. Or that he'd taken up with a different partner and was too afraid to admit it to his wife and many children. Selfishly, Klara hoped he wouldn't show up with that new partner tonight and cause a fuss in the middle of her party.

"Rumor is the lot of them tried to scale Candy Mountain and died," said a man's voice.

Klara placed a hand protectively on Ginger's shoulder and shot a glare at Fritz, who must have let himself in during Ginger's outburst, not even bothering to chime the doorbell. His side-parted hair was slicked against his head, and he wore a tapered black vest over a white shirt. So plain! At least there were little snowflakes embroidered into the vest.

"Don't be insensitive, Fritz!" Klara snapped.

"What?" he said, offended. "Just sharing the news you've surely been too *busy* to hear." The word "busy" was stressed, as though he believed she hadn't been busy at all.

"Malicious gossip is not news," she countered.

Ginger's children had already scattered into the solarium. Klara escorted her to the bathroom, leaving Fritz to hang up his own coat. He was always the most difficult farmer to deal with during the harvests, and no more pleasant any other time of the year. Everyone brought their yield to Silber House to be processed for the quarterly pickup. This was the way it was done, the way it had always been done. Silber House was the only farm with equipment that could sanitize and pack at scale, saving everyone hours of work. Plus, they had the help of the nutcracker androids who sorted out the bad Pirlipat nuts. Everyone's crops got mixed together, and no one else seemed to care. Ever since Klara's parents left, though, Fritz insisted that everything from his orchard be processed and packaged separately.

"Don't pay him any mind," Klara told Ginger.

The doorbell rang just as they reached the bathroom, and Klara raced back toward the foyer, leaving Ginger to clean herself up. If she wasn't there to greet the next group, Fritz might answer the door for her and sour the atmosphere even more than he already had.

The solarium filled with laughter and conversation as the rest of the guests arrived. A lively set of old holiday songs played through the speakers. Couples danced in the center of the room, and a bunch of the children joined hands and ran in a circle chain until they collapsed.

Klara stood by the snack table with Louise and Alicia, surveying the group to account for who had not yet arrived.

"Where is Dross?" she muttered.

"Who?" Louise said as she stuffed a Pirlipat tart into her mouth.

"Elias Drosselmeyer?" Klara said. "The only *Dross* on Eta, I'm pretty sure."

"Possibly in the galaxy," Alicia added.

Louise brushed a crumb from her lips. "Fashionably late, as always."

"He's gone far beyond fashionable. It's going to be too dark soon," Klara declared.

"Too dark for what?" Louise asked, but Klara was already climbing the stairs to the platform she'd set up in front of the south-facing window.

When she turned off the music, the room quieted and all eyes gradually found their way to Klara.

"Welcome to the twenty-fifth Silber House Winter Party!" Klara announced. The crowd whistled and applauded. "As you can see, I chose Christmas for the theme this year, an Earth holiday that many of you remember with great fondness."

"Ha!" Louise barked, and a few people laughed.

"In that spirit, I have a surprise, something I hope you'll *all* appreciate." She stressed the "all", scowling at Louise.

Klara grabbed the curtain tassel, paused for dramatic effect, and then tugged. The curtain fell heavily away from the floor to ceiling window, puddling on the platform.

The space elevator loomed on the horizon, rising into the sky like a massive steel tree. Klara had painted ornaments and a five-pointed star on the glass of the window so that, overlaid, the elevator resembled a giant Christmas tree. The safety lights along the elevator's tethers and cables blinked like decorative candles.

The crowd oohed and awed and applauded. Klara curtsied, the knot of worry at the base of her neck finally untangling. She'd spent so much time running back and forth across the floor to see how it looked from every angle in the room, adjusting and repainting. She'd read in the archives about how the Christmas tree represented life, rebirth, and absolution. Light and hope in the darkness of winter. And the space elevator meant all of those things to the farmers of Eta. The hope that someday they'd be released from this cold, volcanic world to join their friends and families under the sunshine of Petipa Colony.

Just as Klara started to explain these connections, the ceiling lights flickered and a clock chime rang through the speakers. Everyone turned away from Klara and her steel tree. Dross stood in the middle of the solarium, posing theatrically in his yellow frock coat, his hideous hat tipped down to cover his face. Klara sighed. She'd long ago given up trying to convince him to sew or print something new and better; his awful coat was part of the tradition by now. As was using the Silbers' Winter Party to introduce whatever new innovation or invention he'd been working on over the last year. That was as it should be, but he might have let her know when he planned to arrive, rather than barging in to interrupt her moment.

Klara descended the platform to rejoin the crowd. Louise hooked Klara's arm with hers and patted her elbow. "It's a lovely tree. Quite clever, to include the space elevator as a decoration."

Klara grinned and squeezed her arm. "Any idea what Dross is up to this year?" she whispered.

"No clue. But—" She pointed to the six-foot tall wooden box being rolled in behind him by two of the nutcracker androids. "—it looks a good deal more exciting than last year's surprise of a new wind turbine gear design."

Klara affected an imitation of Dross, scrunching up her face and putting a hand in an invisible pocket. "It increased energy efficiency by point-oh-four-seven percent!"

They nearly collapsed on each other in giggles. Dross cleared his throat, his cyborg eye swiveling until it made direct eye contact with Klara. The two women recovered from their fit, standing straight, only the occasional smirk or snort escaping.

"Ms. Silber," Dross boomed. "Will you please assist me?"

"Oh dear," Louise whispered, and they laughed again.

Klara withdrew her arm from Louise's and skipped across the room. He winked at her with his non-cyborg eye and smiled with half his mouth, always the stern uncle with the soft heart. She clasped her hands behind her back and beamed up at him.

"How are those nutcrackers I fashioned for the Silber House factory working out?"

Klara leaned in close enough that the microphone clipped to his frock coat would catch her voice. "They've been positively dreadful lately." The whole room laughed at her honesty. Plenty of them had witnessed her frustration firsthand when they delivered their winter crops. "It's like they've completely forgotten how to sort! We've had to pick the bad nuts out by hand. Oh, do tell me you've fixed them!"

Klara brushed her fingers across the mysterious box.

"Even better." Dross shooed her away from the box, then bowed to the crowd and declared, "Gentlefolk of Eta, I give you... the new and improved nutcracker."

With a puff of smoke and a flourish of his atrocious yellow coat—always the showman, Dross—the walls of the box fell away, revealing a shiny new android. Whereas the original nutcracker androids were short, clunky, faceless robots, this one stood as tall as Dross, dressed in a red coat, trousers trimmed with gold brocade, and the most stylish little black boots.

The oohs and ahhs from the crowd were much more pronounced than for Klara's tree, but she wasn't jealous in the slightest.

"Oh, Dross! He's magnificent!"

"Eighty percent more efficient at sorting, nearly twenty times quicker at adaptive learning, and two-point-eight percent less carbon emissions."

That last point was no small matter—because of Eta's high volcanic activity, they had to be careful their industry wouldn't tip the atmosphere into the same type of run-away greenhouse effect Earth suffered from. Still, Klara rolled her eyes, hoping he wouldn't launch into a dull speech like the wind turbines last year.

Klara strode over and ran a finger playfully across the android's chin. He had the face of an attractive young man, with a sharp nose and thick eyebrows.

"Yes, yes, that's all well and good," Klara said. "But what impresses me is how good-looking you made him." Some wolf-whistles of agreement came from the crowd. The nutcracker stood tall and rigid, eyes still closed.

"Why, Dross," Louise shouted, "the new robot looks just like you did twenty years ago."

"Thirty, maybe," someone else shouted, and that sent the room into hysterics. Dross reddened. Klara shimmied next to the nutcracker to elicit a few more laughs, then stood on her toes to kiss Dross on the cheek.

"Thank you, this is a perfect gift."

Dross set off another smoke bomb to regain the crowd's attention. "This is only the prototype, but within the year, all current nutcrackers will be recycled and replaced with Nutcracker 2.0."

"And then in two years, maybe you'll invent something to benefit the rest of us." The room quieted as attention shifted toward Fritz.

"Fritz," Klara said with a sigh. "Don't make a scene."

"A scene! I apologize, your highness." He affected a mocking bow. "I'd hate to ruin your party by reminding you that other farmers exist."

"A demonstration!" Dross shouted with another burst of smoke, and the nutcracker's eyes popped open.

Klara turned her back on Fritz, shooting him one last glare over her shoulder, and clapped along with the rest of the crowd as the old nutcrackers rolled in a barrel of Pirlipat nuts, and the new nutcracker showed off his skills.

The Battle

Dross put the new nutcracker back into sleep mode and set him between one of the ice sculptures and the banquet table of Pirlipat tarts. Klara made her rounds, the way her parents always had when they'd run this party. While she worked hard to keep the atmosphere festive, somber topics kept creeping in.

Ginger flitted from group to group, asking everyone when they'd last seen her husband. Several other adults had also gone missing without a trace. Theories ranged from the mundane—that they'd fallen into geothermal vents while harvesting radishes—to the conspiratorial—that they had done some favor for the Petipa government and been secretly transported to the Colony—to the fantastic—that massive furry creatures had been sighted, perhaps a type of native animal that was attacking people.

Fritz scoffed. "Oh, don't be absurd, everyone knows there's no large native fauna on Eta."

"*No large native fauna*," Klara repeated in a mocking tone. "Seriously, do you hear yourself sometimes?" To the others, she said, "I hate to admit he's right, of course. The people who say they've seen these creatures have clearly been drinking too much eggnog."

She took a sip of her own nog and winked at Louise, who held a whole handful of Pirlipat tarts in a purple napkin, scarfing one after the other as though she hadn't eaten for a week.

"I'm not so sure," said Pranab. "There's so much of this moon we haven't explored. Who knows what might be lurking out there."

Klara admired his elegant bright blue kurta, but scoffed at his claim. "Something like a giant *rodent* surely would have been noticed in the initial expeditions."

"Not if they hibernate for long periods," Pranab countered. "Maybe they awaken every fifty years, and that's why we're only now seeing them."

"Like cicadas," Alicia said with a punctuating nod.

"Expeditions or not," Pranab continued, "they couldn't possibly have tracked everything that lives on Candy Mountain. No one's ever climbed it."

Fritz opened his mouth, surely to offer his theory that the missing people fell to their deaths doing just that. Klara snatched one of Louise's tarts from the napkin and held it under his nose in the guise of an offering. He frowned, distracted, and took the tart.

"And I suppose you're going to be the first," Alicia said to Pranab. A hint of admiration underlay her teasing.

He struck a pose with one foot up on a chair, planting an imaginary flag. "Before next winter harvest, for king and country."

"Whatever would you want to do that for?" Klara asked.

Candy Mountain was a blight on the horizon, a spire of obsidian and glassy metamorphic rock at the top of the fertile valley, the start of the untraversable volcanic wasteland that made up the majority of Eta.

Pranab started quoting some Earth poet and talking about the thrill of discovery. Fritz wandered away in boredom. *Sorry I asked*, Klara thought as Pranab continued to rhapsodize.

Someone drifted past their group, and Klara did a double-take at an unfamiliar face—feminine with smooth, pale skin, and stark-white hair. Some dancers whirled by, and Klara lost track of the stranger in the crowd.

A stranger! That was impossible—no new farmers had arrived on Eta in ten years, and she knew every child who had been born here.

"Excuse me," Klara said as she slipped away from the group, who still entertained Pranab's absurd plans to scale Candy Mountain. She searched the crowd for that stark-white hair. It must have been a costume, Klara decided, perhaps a wig or a hat made of the same white faux fur as Alicia's coat. Or this might be Benjamin or one of the other missing men, not missing after all but merely trying on a different gender. *Wouldn't that be a delightful twist to this missing persons story!* Klara thought.

But then she caught sight of the stranger again and that notion fled. The white-haired woman was waifish and petite, with the delicate look of a glass doll. Not at all the same body type as Benjamin, nor of most of the robust farmers in the room, regardless of gender. She turned and Klara caught sight of eyes so large and dark they were almost insect-like. Soft pink lips parted in surprise, and the stranger darted into the kitchen, leaving the door swinging behind her.

Klara followed her into the kitchen. A blast of cold air tugged her attention to the back door and Klara glimpsed a snow-white leg and the trail of a diaphanous skirt before the door slammed shut. Klara gathered up her skirt, cursing herself for not cleaning the dirty floor of the mud room.

On the back steps, she rubbed her arms against the brisk cold, scanning the dark trees behind Silber House. A breeze rustled quietly through the Pirlipat orchard. The space elevator blinked in the dark distance. The strange woman she'd followed was nowhere in sight.

Just as she was about to go back inside, Klara heard sounds from amidst the trees: a click, an electronic *zot*, and a muttered curse. With caution, she stepped down to the ground and approached the orchard. Shadows took shape as human figures in the dim light, a few rows in. Not the strange woman, certainly. It looked like—

"*Fritz?*"

Fritz crouched over the new nutcracker with a handheld soldering gun. He looked up at Klara in alarm, dropped the soldering gun into the snow, and scrambled to his feet. The back of the nutcracker's head was left open, circuits exposed.

"Fritz!" Klara shouted as he ran off into the trees. "Fritz, I know that was you. What the hell do you think you're doing?"

She started to chase after him, but then a different voice stopped her in her tracks.

"Hello? Where am I?"

Klara turned on her heel and looked at the nutcracker. He pushed himself up off the ground and lifted a hand to tenderly touch the back of his head.

"Hello, Miss Silber." He blinked at Klara. "I, um, I believe something has happened to me." Then, he laughed. It was a musical sound, charming, yet strange, because androids *didn't* laugh. Klara slowly approached. The nutcracker felt around on the ground until he located the missing plate and attempted to fit it over the exposed wires on the back of his head.

"Here, let me help." Klara took the plate from him, brushed the dirt off the best she could, and deftly fitted the section back onto his head with a quiet snap.

"Thank you." He gazed up at Klara with a sense of wonder in his eyes. "I feel I've just woken up from a very long dream."

"Oh dear," Klara said. Whatever Fritz did must have caused the nutcracker to gain sentience. That happened sometimes—it was becoming increasingly more common back on Earth, if the stories from more recent arrivals were to be believed. But it had never happened with one of the nutcrackers before. "We better get you back to Dross."

She extended a hand. The nutcracker reached out and took it. His hand felt surprisingly warm, not the same cold steel she'd touched during the demonstration.

"Do you have a flashlight function?" Klara asked.

The nutcracker's eyes became beams of light, shining into the orchard like headlights.

"Perfect. Let's get you back inside."

It was closer to go in the back door, but if she took him in the front, more people would notice, and that's exactly what she wanted. She'd already missed enough of her party because of Fritz. She'd deliver the new nutcracker back to Dross and inform him of what Fritz had done in front of everyone. Maybe she'd announce it through the speakers to the whole of Eta. Fritz deserved nothing less.

Light shone from the nutcracker's eyes across the bare winter branches of the Pirlipat trees, making odd shadows dance along the ground. "This place is beautiful," he said.

"Is it?" Klara didn't really think so. She looked for the beauty he spoke of, but saw only the uniform rows of trees her parents planted and left her to tend. The piles of weeds she'd have to burn once the harvest shipment was delivered to the elevator. The tree shaker machine that needed a repair to its tire. The cold hard-packed dirt catching on the hem of her skirt. It was all a means to an end; work she had to complete to be worthy of going on to Petipa Colony, where her real life would begin.

"Quite beautiful," the nutcracker said with a sincere nod.

Klara reached for his hand, hoping to encourage him to walk a little faster, and not trip over his own feet.

As they approached the gate at the far end of the orchard, screams split the night air.

"Stop," she whispered to the nutcracker. The swinging light of his eye beams steadied. She turned him toward the house, to better see. People were leaving the party. Not just leaving—people were *running* out the front door. Klara flung the gate open and raced up the hill toward the house.

"Wait!" Klara shouted, but no one did. She stopped in the driveway, watching in dismay as the cars, tractors, and bicycles parked along the road sped off into the night.

"Klara!" The sound of Fritz's voice sent a surge of anger through her veins. She whirled around, ready to let him know exactly how mad she was.

Outside the front door, Fritz crawled backward on the ground, a hulking shadow looming over him. Klara stumbled backward with a gasp. The nutcracker jogged toward them, his eye beams illuminating the second impossible thing Klara had seen that night.

A giant rat was reared up on its haunches, easily five feet tall with dagger-like teeth. It hissed, yellow eyes half closing as though pained by the light from the nutcracker's eye beams. Fritz grabbed the door frame to haul himself to his feet. His vest was torn and a deep scratch marred his cheek. The rat dropped to all fours and bounded at its new target: Klara and the nutcracker.

Dumbfounded, Klara watched the creature race toward her, but the nutcracker had the sense to step in between them. With surprising agility for an android, he kicked the rat solidly in the chest, sending it flying backward into a tree. The rat rolled over, got back to its feet with a shake and bristle of gray-brown fur, and charged again. This time, the rat caught the nutcracker in a bear hug. He struggled, arms pinned to his sides, but managed to land a kick to the rat's leg with one boot. The rat's grip loosened. The nutcracker grasped the rat by the scruff of the neck and flipped it over onto the ground. It landed with a heavy thud, but grabbed the nutcracker's arm and dragged him down, too. They rolled a few times, down the hill of the driveway, until the rat ended up on top, the nutcracker holding off the attack at arm's length.

Hideous yellow teeth—almost the color of Dross's awful frock coat—gnawed toward the nutcracker's face.

Finally coming to her senses, Klara kicked off one shoe and picked it up. Not much of a weapon, but it was at least heavy and solid. She flung the shoe with impeccable aim, striking the rat right between the eyes. In shock, it let go of the nutcracker and stumbled backward. Back on his feet in no time, the nutcracker sent a pulse of electricity from the palm of his hand.

That's certainly a new feature, Klara marveled.

The rat yelped and limped off into the orchard. The nutcracker started to follow it, but Klara yelled, "Let it go! You've defended us well." He obeyed, dropping to one knee.

Fritz still clung to the doorframe. Klara gathered her shoe and shoved it back on her foot. She tapped the nutcracker on the shoulder. He stood, following her to the house. She grabbed Fritz by the arm to peel him from his frozen state of shock and shoved him into the foyer.

"No large native fauna, right?" she said as she shut and locked the door behind them.

Klara turned, and the wreckage of her party greeted her. The closet spilled over with coats, most of the guests having abandoned theirs when they fled. Half the decorations had been torn down, and all but one of the tables had been upset. Pastries and hors d'oeuvres spilled onto the floor. She blinked away tears.

Now that the threat was gone, Fritz shook out of his stupor, and crushed tarts into the tile with his pacing.

"We have to organize a hunting party immediately," Fritz said. "These creatures are a danger to our community, they must be stopped. You—" He pointed at the nutcracker, still pacing. "Are all the nutcrackers programmed to fight like that?"

"I do not know, sir," the nutcracker responded. "Parts of my programming are based on Earth Private Defense, prototype 154518."

"I don't know what that means," Fritz said. "But we must amass a force to track this creature down, since *somebody* let it get away."

He glared at Klara, but she was hardly even paying attention to him. She sank down in the middle of the solarium floor, her dress pooling around her, and picked up a decorative reindeer. It was missing one leg, its antlers smeared with the golden filling from the Pirlipat tarts. She threw the dumb thing across the room. She wasn't prepared to handle any of this. Her parents left her here alone on this terrible moon, her party had been ruined, and now there were giant rats suddenly terrorizing the valley? Nothing made sense.

"Uh, Klara?" The fire had gone out of Fritz's voice, replaced with an insecure tremor.

"*What?*" she snapped. And on top of everything there was Fritz, with his irrational hatred of Silber House, and his inability to do things the way that worked best for everyone. What had he been *doing* with the new nutcracker out in the orchard, anyway? Klara stood up, ready to tell him just what she thought about him and his tampering, but he wasn't even looking at her. He was pointing toward the kitchen.

The woman Klara had followed earlier stepped daintily from the kitchen into the solarium. Her head swung from side to side, big black eyes taking in the mess. Klara wiped the tears off her cheeks and goggled at the woman. She'd entirely forgotten about the stranger. And this was, indeed, a stranger. She was someone—something—brand new.

Fritz picked up a chair, wielding it over his shoulder like a weapon. The woman took a step back.

"Stop." Klara got to her feet and put a hand on his arm. The woman stood on one leg like a ballerina plucked right out of a child's music box. "She doesn't look like a threat."

"Appearances can be deceiving," Fritz said.

"That's true enough. But we don't need to start this encounter with aggression."

Reluctantly, he lowered the chair. Klara stepped forward.

"Hello, I'm Klara Silber," she said. "Did you see what happened here?" The woman cocked her head, inspecting Klara with those large black eyes. The closer Klara looked, the less human she appeared. What she had first assumed was a diaphanous dress train was in fact a pair of delicate transparent wings. Her silver-white skin had an opalescent shimmer to it, like the carapace of a beetle. Plenty of alien life had been discovered since humans ventured into space, but none so close to human as this.

Klara tried again, pointing at herself and saying, "Klara."

"Klara," the woman repeated, voice high-pitched and wispy like notes on a piccolo. She pointed extraordinarily long fingers at her chest and said something that sounded like, "Plum."

"Plum," Klara said. "Who... what are you?"

Plum suddenly lifted onto the toe of one foot, the other leg hiked and bent in an arabesque, then twirled and dipped, those odd wings swaying behind her. Klara looked back toward Fritz and the nutcracker, who both gaped with confusion. She felt about the same. Plum stopped her dance and spoke a few sounds, punctuated with fluid arm movements, but Klara couldn't decipher what she was saying. She shook her head.

"I'm sorry, I don't understand." She lifted her arms in an exaggerated shrug, hoping that would serve as a universal sign for, "*Huh?*"

Plum grimaced in frustration, then pirouetted toward the door. She took hold of the knob and pulled. Cool night air flowed in, and Plum bowed, sweeping her hand toward the outside.

"I think she wants us to come with her," Klara said.

"No way," Fritz said.

"There are many unknown variables, and the risk is high," the nutcracker said.

"You'll defend me if we run into something scary?" she said with a flirtatious bat of her eyes.

"Of course I will protect you from any threat," he declared. "But I recommend we stay sheltered."

Klara considered him. Why would Dross have used a soldier droid as a basis for an agricultural worker? She'd been so distraught earlier about the party and the giant rat that she hadn't had time to contemplate it. Nor was there any time now, with a strange new friend and a rather important decision to be made.

"What if she leads us right back to that... that *thing*?" Fritz said. "You're going to get us all killed."

"Look," Klara said. "When a fairy shows up and asks you to follow her into the woods, I think you should do it."

"Because nothing bad ever happens to people who do *that* in the old Earth stories." His tone dripped with sarcasm.

"Fine, you two stay here, then. I'm going." Klara grabbed a coat at random off the pile in the foyer closet. It was thick and warm, and reached her knees. She pulled the gray faux fur hood over her head and fastened the oversized buttons.

Her curiosity was genuine, but also, if she delivered news of this historical first contact to Petipa along with this season's harvest, it was a surefire ticket off Eta.

"I advise against this journey," the nutcracker said, "But if you go, I shall accompany you."

Klara reached out with a smile, and he stepped forward to take her hand.

"Do feel free to walk home, Fritz," Klara said. "But take care not to get into a fight with any large fauna on your way. I'm afraid we won't be around to rescue you this time."

Fritz spat a rather vulgar curse, and began digging through the pile of coats, not content to take just any. Klara slipped out the door, the nutcracker and fairy at her side, thinking she'd left Fritz behind. But before they could even make it to the orchard, he appeared, racing to catch up.

Wondrous Things

Plum led the group through the Silber's orchard and past the wintering grain fields, through the wild forest, over a frozen stream and up a boulder-strewn hill. A few of Dross's wind turbines spun in the night breeze at the top of the hill, supplementing the geothermal energy they drew most of their power from. Though they all kept a careful eye on their surroundings, no giant rats ambushed their journey.

Just as Klara started to lament not changing into some more sensible shoes, they approached what looked like a large snowdrift. Then the mound shifted, revealing itself to be made of wings, neck, and beak.

"It's a swan!" Fritz exclaimed.

Perhaps it was, though many times larger than the archive images Klara had seen of swans on Earth. This majestic creature was as wide as a boat, its beak as long as a rake. The neck curved up sinuously as it lifted away from a ruffled white wing.

"No large native—" she started.

"I get it," Fritz snapped. "Clearly there's a lot about Eta that's different than what we thought."

"Clearly," Klara agreed. "Have they only just landed from another world, or have they been hibernating like Pranab suspected?"

"I guess we're about to find out," Fritz said.

The giant swan stretched a wing out and Plum climbed the feathery ramp until she reached an elaborate wooden saddle. She bowed again, inviting the others to join. Klara stepped forward, but Fritz grabbed her coat sleeve and said, "Let the android go first."

Klara yanked her arm free. "He's not just an android. In case you didn't notice, he gained sentience because of whatever you were messing with in his brain."

"I don't mind going first, Ms. Silber," the nutcracker said.

"That's fine," Klara told him. "Go first if it's your choice to, not because this nitwit said to. And don't you dare call me *Ms. Silber* again."

The nutcracker climbed the swan's wing and settled into the second row of seats in the wide saddle. Klara followed, sitting beside him.

"Now that you're, well, *you*, we can't keep calling you 'Nutcracker.' That's not a proper sort of name."

The nutcracker seemed to think about that for a moment. "If you don't mind," he said, "I'd like to be called Nathan."

"Nathan, it is!" she exclaimed.

His whole face lifted with a grin. It was an expression of joy that neither a soldier droid nor an agricultural processing worker had ever been programmed with, something entirely his own.

Fritz took his seat next to Plum, casting a dubious glance at the fairy, who tugged the reins of the giant swan. Klara clutched at Nathan as the swan lifted off the ground, but once they stabilized, she laughed and relaxed. The wind blew her hood back. The swan ascended above the layer of thin clouds and the light reflecting off the distant Petipa was suddenly so bright it almost looked like dawn.

Eta was technically a moon, but it was almost the same size as the planet itself. They both had atmospheres, but Petipa supported little natural vegetation. Eta may have once been green and fertile, until a supervolcano washed lava across most of its land, leaving only one valley a few hundred kilometers long untouched. The habitable area of Eta wasn't large enough to support all the colonists who had left Earth, but Petipa couldn't grow enough food for a colony to survive. And so those who couldn't pay the fee for passage to Petipa farmed this small strip of arable moon-land, and sent it up the space elevator to feed the Colony. How nice it must be, Klara often pondered, to simply enjoy the fruits of this labor instead of toiling for it! She pictured lavish restaurants like in the old Earth movies, and meal parcels delivered to doorsteps by androids much less advanced than Nathan.

The swan flew higher, so much that Klara began to wonder if they would leave the atmosphere and touch the top of the space elevator. But then, the clouds parted, revealing the sheer cliffs and smooth volcanic rock of Candy Mountain, so named for its resemblance to the crystalline sugars of scrumptious hard candies.

A cave greeted them like an open, laughing mouth, and the swan swooped right into it. Though Klara braced for the impact, they landed graceful as a snowflake. Glowing crystals embedded in the cave's roof bathed the area in blue light. Three other swans lifted their heads from slumber to acknowledge their arrival. The area smelled of straw from their roosts; musty yet pleasant.

From his post at the back of the cave, someone in a skin-tight leotard watched them. He had the same shimmering silver skin and stark-white hair as Plum, but whereas Plum was slim and had delicate wings, this man was broad shouldered and barebacked.

Plum leaped from the swan's wing, curtsied to the man and danced some elaborate footwork. Klara held her skirt with one hand and Nathan's arm with the other, watching the interaction as she navigated her way down. Once on solid ground, she turned to say something to Nathan, but he let go of her arm and suddenly pirouetted. The fairies both turned their glassy black eyes toward him. Klara and Fritz glanced at each other with twin expressions of confusion. Then, Plum replicated the movement.

"Um," Klara said after a moment. "What's going on? I mean, it's lovely, and I had no idea you knew ballet, but... what?"

Nathan bowed to the fairies and they bowed back. He turned to Fritz and Klara.

"They communicate through dance," he explained. "I believe if I watch them for an hour or so, I can catalog enough of their movements for functional translation."

"What?" Klara asked.

"Oh!" Fritz said. "Like bees."

"...what?" Klara repeated.

"*Bees*." He spoke with a sense of wonder that Klara had never heard from him before. "An insect pollinator from Earth. Bees communicate partially through a type of dance, making complex movements while they fly to signal information to other bees."

"Huh," Klara said. The universe grew stranger by the moment. She linked her arm with Nathan's, not wanting to be far from him in this unknown environment, beautiful as it was. "And you think you can understand them."

"I've figured out a few phrases already."

"Let's go watch the show then, and find out what kind of a story we've found ourselves in."

Plum motioned for them to follow her again, and this time no one hesitated. The fairies led them through a tunnel, deep inside the mountain.

Geothermal vents heated the passageways, more blue crystals embedded in the walls lighting their way. Klara took off her borrowed coat, draping it over her arm. They wound down a spiral staircase carved into the stone, and after a few minutes found themselves in a larger room, full of plants.

Plants, as a rule, didn't tend to excite Klara. Her livelihood depended on being able to tell a weed from a crop, recognize which were healthy or afflicted with blight. She knew hundreds of both native and imported plants and their specific needs, but they were drab green things; even the white blooms of the Pirlipat trees were noticeable only as a way to evaluate the size of the upcoming harvest. She'd never found them beautiful. This lush garden inside the mountain, however, took her breath away.

Flowering vines scaled the walls with hexagonal blossoms that looked exactly like sugary pastries. A few gnarled trees twisted up toward an open ceiling, where the starry sky peeked in. Despite the open roof, the air around them stayed comfortably warm, like a kitchen after baking a batch of tarts. Pink and green bioluminescent plants sprouted all around Klara, lighting the area with a magical glow.

Plum sat briefly on a white cushion and then hopped up and gestured for Klara and Nathan to take her place. Klara prodded the seat with her fingertips before sitting down.

"I believe this is a mushroom! Some kind of fruiting body, anyway." She flopped down onto it and arranged her skirt around her legs. "Oh, it's all so lovely! I wish everyone was here. This would be a wonderful setting for a party." Her smile dimmed. After what happened, there may be no party next year. She wasn't here for decorative inspiration; she was here to find answers about why there were suddenly fairies and swans and murderous giant rats running amok on Eta.

Nathan sat to her right, and Fritz chose a different mushroom seat a few feet away. A dozen fairies trailed out into the meadow before them. Their wings were tinted the same pale blue as the glowing crystals Klara had seen in the cave tunnels. Plum danced a message to them. Klara looked up at Nathan. He smiled down at her, but kept his eyes trained on the fairies. He was the key to finding out what was happening. Nothing to do about any of it until then. Might as well watch and enjoy.

And watch they did. The fairies leapt and twirled around the leaf-strewn clearing. First Plum alone, then a man joined her. Then a different pair, who moved in slow, sensuous unison. Though no traditional music played, they did not dance in silence. Harmonizing together, the alien vocalizations of the fairies sounded like the chords of a violin, the whistles of a flute, the chime of a triangle. Several groups came and went, some of their dances lively, some of them somber, all of them elaborate and striking. Patterns and adornments marked the costumes of many of the dancers, and Klara wondered if they were tribal affiliations. She noted at least four distinct groups, if so.

Klara sneaked occasional glances at Nathan, imagining the calculations going on in his newly sentient mind. It would be a crime if Dross reprogrammed him after all this. She wouldn't let that happen. Gaining sentience might have been an accident, but miracles often were. He was awake now, and he deserved life and love like anyone else.

The dancers bowed and Fritz applauded, then stopped himself. He shoved his hands into his pockets, embarrassed, and slouched on his mushroom cushion.

"And to think, you didn't even want to come," Klara teased.

Nathan rose and danced a few steps with Plum.

"So, do you understand them?" Klara asked once he finished.

"I do," Nathan said. "But I have to warn you, it is not a happy story."

"Then best to tell it quickly. Break our hearts as soon as possible so we have time to heal."

"Long ago," Nathan started, "there were many more of them. They spread to every corner of this world, but strife brewed between the clans. During a great war, the Inks clan deployed a weapon that triggered a volcanic eruption so colossal it engulfed most of the world. Forced into closer proximity in the fertile valley, conflicts continued to trouble the clans. Beings from other worlds visited from time to time, and one of these visitors bestowed upon them a sacred nut. When they learned what it could do, they established a ritual to foster alliances that would mend their divides. Youth joined a clan based on the outcome of a ritual battle, rather than remain with the clan they were born into."

"You got all this from some fancy footwork," Fritz said, skeptical.

"Yes," Nathan replied, unfazed by the skepticism.

"A sacred nut?" Klara asked.

"Yes. A mutation of the Pirlipat nut tree, which in turn caused a temporary mutation of their bodies in preparation for the ritual battle."

"A mutation..." Klara repeated. "You mean the bad nuts. The ones you... the ones the nutcrackers were designed to sort out."

"The mutagenic effects of the sacred nut were temporary," Nathan continued, "and the youth would join their new clan and live peacefully until the next generation. But then one year, the transformations were more extreme, and those who transformed did not return to their original form. Rather than battle according to the ritual, they attacked the spectators. Many were killed, and the ritual abandoned. The survivors retreated to this mountain. The corrupted ran wild in the fertile valley until they died out."

"The rat creature that attacked us," Klara reasoned. "We've been having trouble recently sorting out the bad nuts. If some got through..." She thought of the Pirlipat nut pastries arranged artfully on the buffet tables at the party, and gasped in horror. "It wasn't a large native fauna at all! That creature could have been any one of my guests who were unlucky enough to eat a tart made from the wrong nuts."

Not to mention Benjamin and the others who had gone missing—is that what happened to them? They might be out there in the forest transformed, confused, and dangerous.

Nathan danced this theory to Plum, and then nodded to Klara. "Your hypothesis seems likely."

Klara frowned. "But why *now*? Why was it just this year's harvest that the bad nuts began to slip through?" This was the first winter harvest since her parents left, but she'd run the factory exactly the same as they used to, so she couldn't imagine it was any fault of her own. She huffed. "The nutcrackers *are* getting older. Maybe they got overwhelmed. The farmers have gotten too dependent on them, I bet they didn't do sufficient pre sorting—"

"Oh, don't you dare blame the other farmers," Fritz blurted. Klara and Nathan both turned to stare at him. He hunched down on the mushroom cushion, arms crossed and messy hair falling across his eyes.

"Then what?" Klara asked with an exasperated shrug. "Are you suggesting it was another mutation like when their ritual failed? That would be quite the coincidence."

Fritz squirmed for a moment before he said, "It was me."

An awkward silence greeted his pronouncement. "Sorry, say that again?" Klara said after a moment.

"Yes." Fritz threw his arms wide, fixing Klara with a defiant stare. "I did it. I compromised the old nutcrackers. I changed their programming so the bad nuts would slip through."

That must have been what he was attempting to do with Nathan as well, Klara supposed. She shook her head. "But Fritz, *why*?"

His face burned red, and he resembled nothing more than a child about to throw a tantrum.

"Silber House has too much... too much *power*," he finally spat out. "You've made the rest of us dependent on your factory, and when the harvest goes up to Petipa with the Silber House labels slapped on everything, it looks like you're responsible for *all* of it. Your parents didn't get the invitation because of their own hard work. They got it by exploiting the rest of us."

"*That's* why you've hassled us to process and package yours separately? And you sabotaged the nutcrackers in order to, what, ruin Silber House's reputation and elevate yourself?"

"How else are any of us supposed to get ahead when the system is set up to always keep us behind?"

Klara's ears burned, her jaw clenched. "You could have killed someone with this scheme of yours. If the bad nuts affect people the way we've just heard, you may have. You understand that, right?"

Fritz blanched. "I didn't know anything about that, of course. I... I thought it would be like a mild food poisoning. Maybe an allergic reaction. Just enough to make you look bad. To... to make it so Petipa would order you to change your operations and the rest of us could have some equity. Who knew that the nuts could actually transform people into... into..."

He trailed off, looking toward the fairies, huddled together watching their argument with wide, terrified eyes.

"Into large native fauna," he finished pitifully.

Klara crossed her arms and stared at him, waiting for him to offer an apology for the damage he'd done to her orchard, to the party, to the coming harvest. He only stared back defiantly and after a moment, she threw her hands up.

The fairies were dancing again.

"There's more," Nathan said. His gaze darted across the ensemble, calculating the meaning of their movements.

Klara glanced between the nutcracker and the dancers. This piece seemed to be dominated by one particular clan, limbs decorated in green leaf tattoos, who moved in a sharp, athletic manner. A sense of violence pervaded the dance.

"What are they saying?" she whispered to Nathan, when he didn't immediately offer an interpretation.

"The sacred nuts can be returned to their true nature by a man with a ten-season beard... who walks seven steps backward... and breeds a nut that cannot be cracked... I'm not sure I'm getting all of this correctly; it seems nonsensical."

"A metaphor?" Klara guessed. "Some parable in their folklore?"

"It must be."

Plum joined the stage again, and after a moment, the nutcracker said, "Ah, I understand now. They have developed an antidote from a flower grown in these mountains, something that should reverse the transformation."

"Great!" Klara nearly shouted.

"Some of them wish to share this antidote with the humans, now that they've observed the transformations affecting your community."

"Even more great!"

"Some of them do not."

"Oh. That's... not so great."

Nathan danced a question, but then frowned as he translated the answer.

"The Inks clan claim that before the fateful winter harvest when the transformations would not reverse, new stars began appearing in the sky. Unknown visitors who would not greet them were seen lurking near the Pirlipat trees with... with a single eye for a head."

"A single eye for a head?" Klara said in disbelief. Were even more strange creatures lurking in the shadows of Eta?

Fritz grimaced. "I think I understand. The helmets on exploration suits."

"Us, you mean," Klara said. "Or, rather, the Earth explorers who decided Eta should be Petipa's breadbasket." She chewed on that devastating possibility for a long moment.

"They..." The dance concluded and Nathan turned to her, his face creased with concern. "The Inks—the ones who don't want to share the antidote—they plan to destroy the space elevator, to ensure no more of your kind arrive."

Klara blew out a deep breath. "Well. That's no good."

Tens of thousands of people in Petipa Colony depended on the food they grew on Eta and sent up the space elevator. To destroy the elevator would be responding to one genocide by initiating another one. Not to mention that it would mean everyone here who had worked their lives away for the chance to join the Colony would be stuck on Eta indefinitely.

"Explain to them that we're refugees, please," Klara said. "Those of us who live here, our families had to flee our dying homeworld. If something was done to the trees here before we arrived, we knew nothing of it."

"Some of them are sympathetic," Nathan said after he'd delivered the message. "They have quite a lot of disagreement about humans overall, but most do not support the destruction of the space elevator. That's why Plum sought out your party and brought us here."

Klara smiled at Plum, but when the fairy attempted a smile back, the effect was to display a mouthful of jagged teeth, like the mandibles of a beetle. Klara set her discomfort aside. She shouldn't judge something non-human by the standards of human beauty—and even within those standards, Plum was still quite beautiful, razor teeth notwithstanding. And if the founders of Eta and Petipa truly had done what the fairies claimed, then humans were more monsters than either fairy or giant rat.

The mushroom cushion suddenly became very uncomfortable. Klara abandoned it and paced while she tried to think of a solution, but no quick fix was evident. She clung to Nathan's arm and looked up desperately into his face. "Can you please ask them what their demands are?"

He nodded, and she forced herself to let go so he could dance the question to them.

Klara couldn't understand the fairies' dance language, but she could tell an argument when she saw one. This wasn't going anywhere, and she was becoming uncomfortably aware of how the dancers now encircled the three of them.

"Are they even going to let us leave?" Klara asked.

"Some believe the humans are harmless, that it was some other being who corrupted the Pirlipat. Plum has compared you to an adorable doll."

"That's... flattering, I suppose," Klara said.

"But some of them believe it would be prudent to hold us prisoner until after the space elevator is destroyed."

"*Prudent*," Klara repeated. "They'll start a war this way."

Fritz scoffed. "You think the other farmers will charge up here into battle just because a *Silber* has been kidnapped?"

"You don't think all of us would rally to rescue any of us that are kept in danger?"

Fritz's eyes darted away in embarrassment, and when he spoke, his voice was nearly a whine. "They don't even know we're here."

"That's true," Klara admitted. "And what I meant in the first place was that they'll respond to the sabotage of the elevator by declaring war on the saboteurs. We'll lose any chance of peaceful negotiation or coexistence."

"What do you propose we do?" Nathan asked. He and Fritz watched her expectantly, and all the fairies' eyes were locked on her too.

Klara cleared her throat and stood tall, the way she'd watched her parents do whenever they addressed the other farmers.

"Tell them if they share the antidote and leave the elevator alone, we can reverse the damage done to the sacred nuts of the Pirlipat tree. We will return them to their original potency, so the tradition of ritual battle can resume."

"You don't know how to do that," Fritz hissed.

"Dross does." She had no idea if that was true. But if anyone *could* do it, it would be Dross. "If ever there was a man with a ten-season beard like in their parable, that's Elias Drosselmeyer. Let us go, and Dross will create not just an antidote, but a true cure."

Nathan's mechanical face betrayed some skepticism, but he delivered the message. After some discussion, he told Klara, "They will not hand over the antidote yet."

"But Dross will surely need their sample in order to engineer a more comprehensive one," Klara argued.

"The Inks refuse to compromise on that. But you may return home. Plum must accompany you."

"I would be delighted to have Miss Plum as my houseguest," Klara said. "Wait." Dread sent chills down her arms, despite the geothermally heated air. "Why did you say 'you' instead of 'us'?"

Nathan looked pained. "They are requiring me to stay with them, as collateral."

"No," Klara said. "Absolutely not."

"It will be alright, Klara," he said, though she could see fear evident on his face.

"There must be another way. You're the only one of us who can communicate with Plum!"

Nathan danced her opposition, but the fairies had made up their mind. The nutcracker was to remain at Candy Mountain until the corruption was reversed, and in turn they would delay the destruction of the space elevator. For how long remained unclear.

Klara hugged Nathan with a resigned sigh, and glanced back at him over her shoulder as she, Fritz, and Plum left the garden to traverse through the dark tunnels of the mountain. The swan waited for them where they'd left it, head tucked under its wing in rest.

The wonder Klara felt during the first swan ride was buried now beneath the weight of what she'd learned. Could the government of Petipa have known the fairies lived on Eta? Were they the ones who altered the Pirlipat nuts? She couldn't fathom it. Too much strangeness had infected this night.

This simple world wasn't so simple after all.

The swan delivered them right to the front door of Silber House. As soon as Klara, Fritz, and Plum climbed out of the saddle, it took off again, blending into the dark sky like a cloud drifting toward the horizon.

Klara didn't even bother to kick the snow and mud off her boots. The house was already a disaster. She marched straight across the solarium to the kitchen, ignoring the torn decorations and overturned tables.

To her surprise, Fritz followed her inside. He lingered by the kitchen door while she used the cross-farm intercom on the kitchen wall to dial Dross's code. What was Fritz doing, waiting for her to offer him a ride home? This whole mess was his fault, and she'd much prefer to clean it up without him.

Dross didn't answer, so she left a message.

"Get online, Dross, I have a lot to tell you. A *lot*."

Where else might he be? Some of the older farmers talked about how on Earth, they carried around devices that let them communicate instantly with anyone else on the planet. But on a world with only a few hundred people spread out over a few hundred square miles, where life revolved around the slow growth of their crops, it hadn't been a priority to keep everyone so urgently connected. An intercom system linked each of the barns and farmhouses. But no one carried around pocket computers or wore watches or pins they could speak into like her parents told her had been ubiquitous back on Earth.

Unable to narrow down Dross's whereabouts, she started at the top of the alphabet. Alicia appeared on the screen almost immediately. She'd changed out of her party dress into flannel pajamas.

"Oh, Klara, it was terrible," she wailed. Her eyes were red and puffy. "Worst Silber party *ever*."

That stung. Even as she realized how silly it was to take offense, with everything that had happened and so much else at stake, it still hurt. She'd put a lot of love and effort into that party, and meant only good with it. Rituals, holidays, celebrations: these were important markers that held their community together. How dull life would be without them. Besides, if Fritz hadn't sabotaged the nutcracker androids, then no giant rats would have attacked. Without him, her party would've been just fine.

Klara steeled herself against this flood of emotions. "I didn't see exactly what happened," she said to Alicia. "Are you okay?"

"No! I mean, relatively, I guess. Louise, she—we were talking and eating, and then she just went werewolf. Or, were-rat? She threw the table, and started attacking people. It was a stampede, trying to get out."

Oh, not Louise! She'd been eating handfuls of the Pirlipat tarts. One of them must have contained the bad nuts. Klara shook her head. "Was anyone hurt?"

Alicia started a litany of scratches and bruises and torn clothes and stubbed toes, so Klara revised her question.

"Was anyone killed?"

"No, not that I've heard."

"And Dross, have you—"

But just then, the screen blinked with an incoming call.

"Everything's going to be fine," she told Alicia, and hung up before she could say anything else.

Dross was too close to the camera, his heavy breath fogging up the lens.

"Klara! I'm so sorry—I ran like a coward."

"That's alright, Dross. Are you okay?"

"The creature followed me. I thought I was free of it, but it followed me home. I've trapped it inside the chicken coop."

"Did you kill it?"

"No."

"Good. Don't, if you can help it. I'm coming over."

Klara hung up and turned to see Fritz still lingering in the doorway. If he was going to hang around, he might as well be useful.

"Did you drive here?"

His brow crunched in puzzlement. "Bike."

"Your cargo bike?"

"It's too much hassle to unhook the trailer just to go—"

Klara cut him off with a sigh. "It'll have to do. Dross is only a couple of miles away." She stomped out in search of the bike before waiting for him to agree.

Plum was happy to fly alongside them. Klara tried balancing on the handlebars, but fell three times before they reached the first hill. She climbed into the dusty cargo box and hunkered down, teeth rattling, as Fritz pedaled down the bumpy dirt road.

The Tale of the Hard Nut

D ross still wore the yellow frock coat, now tattered and wet. His beard stuck out in wild clumps, and his hair had broken free of its styling gel into a frizzy mess. Plum twirled behind Klara, possibly trying to tell her something she couldn't understand. She wished Nathan were here. Plum came to a sudden stop the second Dross opened the door, her wings and gown still swaying with momentum. She leaped theatrically sideways to hide behind Fritz.

Dross looked right past Klara to stare at the fairy. His cyborg eye whirred in its socket. "It's not possible. I believed their race to be extinct."

Klara didn't realize the knot of anxiety in her stomach could wind any tighter, but there it went, a full extra loop. "You *knew*."

Sadness flickered across his face. "Please," he said. "Come inside." Klara hurried in, grateful for the indoor warmth. Fritz followed, but Plum lingered outside. She made a squawk like a French Horn, and then tiptoed out of sight. Klara cinched her coat around her waist and left the welcome warmth to follow Plum around the side of the house.

She couldn't see what Plum was looking at in the starlight until Dross came up behind them holding a lantern. The rat creature lay in the chicken coop, heavy breath pulsing its ribcage. It had disposed of the chickens, leaving a mess of feathers and blood everywhere.

A scrap of yellow fabric wrapped around the creature's shoulder. And the more she looked, the more of the fabric Klara spotted, stretched and wrapped around its limbs, crisscrossed over the fur of its back. The same color as Dross's hideous frock coat, she thought at first. But also, the same color as Louise's flapper dress.

"I administered a sedative," Dross said. "Nearly had my arm ripped off in the process." He rolled his right shoulder and winced.

"It's Louise," Klara informed him.

"Yes, the creature must have torn her to shreds," Dross said.

"No," Klara said. "I mean the creature *is* Louise... transformed."

Dross frowned, cyborg eye searching the creature as if he could find Louise's facial features in the lump of fur before him. "It's not possible."

"You said that about the fairies, and yet clearly impossibility abounds this evening."

"Fairies?" Dross asked.

Klara shrugged. "I'm sure they have their own name for themselves, but I don't know how to pronounce—" She swept her arms up and gave a graceless spin. "—or whatever." Plum gave her a horrified look, and Klara crossed her arms, feeling sheepish. She'd probably said something vulgar in their dance language. She cleared her throat. "These impossibilities are connected. I'll explain what I know inside. But, Dross, it's freezing out here. We'll secure her in a locked room inside. It's much more humane."

Dross protested, but Klara was already opening the door of the chicken coop. After a few awkward attempts to lift the creatures, Klara located a tarp and rolled the rat's sleeping body onto it. Klara and Dross dragged the tarp together while Plum flitted ahead to open the door. Fritz gaped in surprise to see them awkwardly maneuvering the rat into the house, but rushed forward to make sure the tail didn't get shut in the door.

Dross opened and closed his hands, rubbing at the wrist, and gratefully let Fritz take the tarp. "Will the pantry suffice? It'll be far more secure than the bedroom, and I'd rather not lose access to the bathroom."

Fritz dragged the tarp in that direction. Klara tossed out pans and sacks of dried summer beans to make space. Once they'd fit the rat into the pantry, Klara started to close the door.

Fritz held up a hand. "Wait a second."

He pulled a blanket off Dross's couch and tossed it on top of the sleeping rat. At last, they locked the pantry door, then piled the heavy sacks of beans against it.

The long night and unexpected labor was catching up with Klara. She kicked off her shoes and flopped onto her back on the couch, throwing an arm over her aching eyes. At least feeling was tingling back into her frozen fingers and ears. A grandfather clock chimed and Klara lost herself in the hypnotic sound, losing track of how many times it gonged.

"I believe some explanations are in order?" Dross said once the clock quieted.

As much as she might want to keep drifting away, sleep still seemed a distant prospect. Klara sucked in a sharp breath of the warm air, and sat up to make space for Fritz. He sat beside her on the couch, hands clasped in his lap, shoulders tense. Plum tiptoed about, inspecting the Earth artifacts that lined Dross's shelves.

"Some of the fairies told us a story I don't want to believe." Her throat felt tight. "First, tell me what you know."

Dross shrugged out of his yellow frock coat, inspecting it as if he just realized how soaked and dirty it had become.

He laid the coat in front of the closet's geothermal wall vent to dry. Still crouched there with his back to Klara, he said, "I was never supposed to come to Eta." He took a seat on the floor, leaning wearily against the wall. His knees tented up, bones pushing against the thin fabric of his trousers. "My passage was fully paid for because my engineering skills were in demand. I boarded the first passenger ship to leave Earth—convinced that I was leaving nothing behind and had only promises ahead—but I was alone. My family had perished in one of the great floods while I was away at school on higher grounds."

He stared at the floor, lost in the tragic memory. Klara felt a pinch of shame that she'd never once considered why Dross had been sentenced to remain on Eta into his old age when so many others were eventually granted an invitation to the Colony.

"The journey from Earth to Petipa took six years back then, and in that time, I thought I'd found a new family among my shipmates. I fell in love. A young man with a brilliant mind, Wendell Confectioner. We were to be married as soon as we reached Petipa. We waited only so we could declare ourselves the first couple to wed on the soil of our new homeland. But then, approximately two years out from landing, we began receiving news from the science vessel that preceded us—bad news about failing crops and toxic soil. It seemed our Colony was doomed before it was ever established."

Plum perched now on the arm of the sofa, close enough that Klara could feel the gentle vibration of her wings, even though they were folded in, tucked nearly out of sight. The fairy listened to Dross's story, though she almost certainly couldn't understand the words. *Perhaps it sounds like a song to her*, Klara thought, *the way her language looks like a dance to us.*

"Everyone on the ship had some form of scientific training, and we dedicated ourselves to working through the problems they sent, hoping a solution could be found by the time we reached our promised home. Breakthroughs were limited by the long transmission times, but we worked tirelessly with a renewed sense of purpose. I was designing a modified version of the aquaponics system the ship used. Simple, yet complex because of the chemical makeup of Petipa's natural groundwater. Everything changed when I discovered Wendell's project."

The lines in Dross's face deepened, skin pulled taut by a grimace.

"It wasn't only him, of course. But he was the one I heard it from, wheedling out the classified information through pillow talk, in some of the last intimate moments we ever shared. Expeditions were being sent to explore the moon, Eta. It had been well-known since before any human stepped foot on either world that there was not enough habitable land on Eta to support a colony the size we had been promised. But reports from those emergency expeditions showed something we couldn't tell from satellite imagery: Eta had large insect-like native life."

"The fairies," Klara supplied.

"They had some other name for them at the time, but yes. The fairies. It was unclear if they were sapient, though plenty of evidence indicated they were." He glanced mournfully up at Plum, who offered no reaction. Dross took a shuddering breath before he went on. "The Pirlipat trees native to Eta were considered a life-saving discovery—edible, nutritious, and able to withstand the hardship of transportation. Wendell sequenced the trees' genome and discovered a natural mutation. He suggested a chemical treatment to the roots that would make just enough of a difference to increase the frequency and severity of that mutation in the edible seed, in order to cull the numbers of the insect population that fed on it. He insisted the intention was not genocide, merely a little pest control so we could more easily cultivate the land. I was appalled, either way. Petipa was desperate, but how could we act so rashly and inhumanely to the first non-human creatures we encountered?

"I demanded he cease working on the project, but he refused. *A strategic sacrifice to ensure our survival in the universe,* he called it. An utter travesty and violation of human progress, *I* thought. I told everyone on the ship what was being done, and was court-martialed for leaking classified plans. I spent my first year on Petipa not honeymooning with my love and working to build our Colony as I'd expected, but locked away like a dangerous animal. Until I was sent here, to Eta. I never knew exactly what happened, only that the insect-like creatures—the, uh, fairies—were mostly gone by the time I arrived. I saw a few glimpses during the first couple of years, but never since then."

"We've brought it all with us," Klara said after a long, quiet moment. "They promised it would be different than it was on Earth, but nothing is different. We've recreated the same terrible history on a different world. I wish we'd done it differently. We should have worked together with the fairies, not just taken over their land."

"What we should have done is fixed the problems back on Earth so that so many of us weren't forced into finding new land in the first place," Dross said. "But I'm afraid that ship sailed long before the first spaceship launched."

Klara didn't entirely understand the metaphor he used, but she resonated with the sentiment.

Where should the chain of apologies start, and what good would any of them do? They needed action, but Klara felt as frozen as the ground outside. She stared into the glass face of the grandfather clock, the optimistic messages of the old propaganda films that had recruited her parents swirling across her mind's eye like rainbows in an oil slick. Klara had watched them many times in the archives, believing every word.

"But you, my dear, have given me hope," Dross said.

Klara blinked back to the present moment to see that he wasn't talking to her, but to Plum. Her wings unfurled as she became aware of his attention, and her dark eyes darted between Klara and Dross. Klara wished she knew a way to tell Plum that Dross meant her no harm. Among all the uncertainties in the world right now, that was one thing she knew was certain.

"Are there many left?" Dross asked Klara.

"I saw a few dozen hiding inside some caves in Candy Mountain. They spoke of clans, so there are likely more."

She shifted her weight on the couch and accidentally brushed Fritz's arm. He'd been so quiet during Dross's story that she forgot he was even there. Remembering his presence enraged her all over again and she scooted further away from him.

"Tell him what you did," she demanded. "To the nutcracker androids at the Silber House factory. Tell him what you did. And what it caused."

Fritz started to protest, but quickly yielded, admitting to Dross how he'd tampered with the nutcrackers. Klara took up the story then and summarized what they'd learned from the fairies about the mutagenic effects of the Pirlipat nuts, and about the Inks clan's threat to destroy the space elevator.

"Oh, Dross, what are we going to *do*?" Klara wailed in despair once she finished the recap.

"First," Dross said, "we need to re-sort the whole Pirlipat harvest."

Dread settled in her stomach as she realized the truth of what he said. If the bad nuts got through to Petipa, it would be a disaster. The giant rats would overrun the dense cities and put everyone in danger. A slaughter, that's what it would be. The end of Petipa Colony and of humanity's hope of thriving on new worlds.

But there wasn't *time* to re-sort the whole harvest. The ship would anchor at the top of the space elevator in only a few days. Klara had never felt so overwhelmed in her life. Not even when her parents ascended the steel tree and left her in charge of the farm and all its complexities. The enormity of this situation and its far-reaching consequences was more than she could process at the moment. Her mind clogged up like the machines when they poured in too many nuts at once.

Klara gasped, recalling a crucial piece of the story she'd left out. "They—oh, Dross, they kept the nutcracker!"

Dross shrugged. "That's unfortunate, but I can make more."

"No!" Klara said. "No, you don't understand! Fritz tinkered with his circuits and woke him up." Fritz gave her a betrayed look. She threw her hands up. "Well, what do you want me to say? You did. And he can speak to them, he can translate their dance language. He's—he's a *person* now, and his name is Nathan, and we have to save him, and we have to save everyone, and we have to make things right, and…"

Klara was on the verge of hyperventilating. Her vision blurred, her breath came sharp and fast.

"Shh, shh," Dross said. He took Fritz's place on the couch and cradled her head to his chest like she was a child. A surge of longing coursed through her, for the comforting touch of her own father, for the lullabies he used to sing to her. But Dross comforted her too, ancient Dross with his deep-lined weathered face and cyborg eye, the kind uncle who cared for everyone on Eta, and for Klara most of all.

"They kept him because *she* promised you could fix it," Fritz said, narrowing his eyes at Klara.

She lifted her head from Dross's chest, face beseeching. "I did promise that," she said. "Can you do it? Do you know enough about what Wendell did to the Pirlipat trees to be able to reverse it?"

Dross's lips curled down as he shook his head, but then said, "I'll see what I can do."

———◆◇◆———

Klara awoke with a foul taste in her mouth, a crick in her neck, and an overwhelming sense of dread at the realization that all the rats and fairies and hidden histories were not, in fact, an elaborate dream. She'd fallen asleep on Dross's couch. The bunched-up velvet of her party dress left creases in the skin of her arms and legs. She smoothed out the fabric, noticing stains and tears collected during the previous night's adventures.

When her parents were still on Eta, the day after the Silber House party was always a day of hard work, removing decorations and cleaning up the remnants of the festivities. Klara was used to hard work, whether in the fields and orchards, in the factory, or scrubbing the floors of the house. But this morning, waking up alone, in the aftermath of the party's disruption and the revelation of the fairies' plight, the amount of work ahead of her was a mountain she couldn't imagine climbing. She pressed a pillow to her face and fell over onto the couch, wishing she could hide in sleep a little while longer.

"Fritz went home," Dross said.

"Thank goodness," Klara said, voice muffled by the pillow. She removed the obstruction and sat up. "I spent more time with him yesterday than I have my entire life. Which is not an experience I'd like to make a regular habit of."

Dross sat in a chair across from her, sipping at a steaming mug. "Then I'm sorry to say he's asked that you meet him at the factory later this morning. Plum went with him."

Klara groaned, but this was good news. "He's fixing the nutcrackers he tampered with?"

Dross nodded.

"I should get out there, then."

Klara stood, but before she could take a single step, Dross held out a bundle to her, which her bleary morning eyes eventually interpreted to be a fresh set of work clothes.

"After breakfast," he said with a kind smile.

Klara changed out of her party dress and then joined Dross in a kitchen that was much smaller than the one in Silber House. She ravaged the jams and breads and fruits he'd set out—not a single Pirlipat nut to be seen in any of them, she noted with relief. It would have been a lovely breakfast if not for the thumps and mewls coming from the giant rat trapped in the pantry. Finally, feeling stronger, and slightly less overwhelmed, Klara and Dross trekked together over to the Silber House processing plant.

Fritz had the nutcrackers all lined up like a platoon, and he was in no more mood to talk to Klara than she to him. While he and Dross tinkered with the androids, she went to the intercom, choosing the one on the second floor that had the fewest sticky buttons and scratches on the lens.

With the "Emergency Recall" tag, she sent a message to every other intercom on Eta, requesting everyone immediately return to the plant whatever allotment of Pirlipat nuts they had taken from the harvest. Then she leaned against the wall and closed her eyes, taking a few deep breaths before everyone began to arrive.

Klara's mother took no guff from the other farmers, and Klara tried to summon that same trait within herself. Her father was always cheerful, even in the face of hardships that drove most people to anger and despair. She searched for that in herself as well, wrapping the two into a shield around her heart.

"Klara? Are you here?"

Her eyes flew open. Alicia was downstairs, calling for her. Klara rushed to the railing and looked down to see Alicia clutching a five-pound mesh bag of nuts. *First to the party, as always,* Klara thought, then frowned when she remembered it had in fact been Louise who arrived first last night. Louise, now trapped in fur and fangs, held prisoner in Dross's kitchen pantry until a solution could be reached with the fairies who held the antidote to her transformation.

One problem at a time. They'd deal with the problem of the Pirlipat harvest first, then they'd sort out the problems with the fairies.

Klara hurried down the stairs to greet Alicia. A few others arrived close behind her. Klara quickly filled them in on the basic details of the mutagenic effect of the bad nuts and the existence of the fairies. More of the Eta farmers arrived while she explained, gathering around to catch what they could of the story. Dross joined the group, leaning against one of the shut-down conveyors. Klara told the others of a scientist who manipulated the Pirlipat trees, but left out

Dross's connection to the man. That would be his story to tell, if he ever chose to.

"We have to re-sort the entire Pirlipat harvest," she ended with a weary shake of her head.

"There's less than a week before the ship docks at the elevator!" Alicia said. "We can't possibly manage it."

"We must," Dross said. "We can't lose any more of our people to the transformation, and we can't risk a replication of Klara's tragic party in the streets of Petipa."

"If everyone works together, we can manage it just fine," Klara said with more conviction in her voice than she really felt. She looked at the crowd before her, the same people who had arrived at Silber House for the celebration last night in their finest new clothing, now gathered in the dusty factory wearing their usual rags. She knew every one of their faces, but she rarely saw so many of them together like this, except during the annual Winter Party. Those faces weren't looking at her with the same respect and admiration they used to show Klara's parents. They were looking at her with scorn, contempt, and even worse: pity.

The nuts wouldn't have to go through the entire lengthy processing again—they were already hulled, cleaned, and pasteurized. Despite the nickname they'd given the androids, the nutcrackers didn't actually crack the nuts—Pirlipat nuts were sent to Petipa with their inner shell intact to preserve freshness—but they were programmed to hand-sort the mutated nuts before packaging. To sort out everything the nutcrackers missed because of Fritz's tampering, they needed every functioning nutcracker on that task, which meant Klara needed as many human hands as possible to haul out what had already been packaged into ration bags and load them onto the conveyor belts, and then load the re-packaged bags onto the trucks that would transport them to the space elevator in only a couple of days' time.

Just as Klara opened her mouth to attempt to rally the farmers to this important task, Plum came dancing toward them with a high-pitched squeak. Even though Klara couldn't understand this dance-language the way Nathan did, it was still clear that something was very wrong. Her appearance sent a ripple of murmurs among the farmers, those who had heard the part of the story about the fairies filling in those who had arrived later.

What has Fritz done now? Klara hurried after Plum into the factory's storage room, where the ration bags were held. Perhaps he'd accidentally granted sentience to all of the nutcrackers and they'd run off in fear and confusion at their newfound awareness. Or he'd sparked a fire in one of their heads and set the whole harvest ablaze.

But what greeted Klara when she finally reached the storage room was not a disaster—at least, not an apparent one. Fritz worked alongside the dozen nutcrackers, hauling bags. It took a moment for Klara to realize he was separating out the bags from his orchard.

"Fritz, we don't have time for this nonsense."

He paused only long enough to jab a finger in her direction. "It is *not* nonsense. I'm done with you taking credit for everyone else's labor."

"We'll leave the Silber House labels off of *all* the bags. One less step that will save us some time anyway."

"That's not the point."

"Isn't it? Look, we can talk about a more equitable packaging system, or alternative ways to convey our contributions once we're not faced with such urgency."

Fritz hadn't paused, nor had the nutcrackers, and a sheen of sweat started to break out across his forehead.

"You need to understand, Klara Silber," he said, voice low and dark, "that you are not actually the one in charge. My yields have fewer of the bad nuts in them anyway, and that's a fact."

Klara lost patience. She marched over and intercepted the bag he'd picked up, hefting it back onto the pile. A nutcracker picked it up nearly as soon as it landed, never pausing from their assignment.

"Fritz, you accuse my family of exploiting you, and the fairies blame the farmers for forcing them off their lands, and maybe those things are true, but *all* of us are at the mercy of some government goons who don't have to live with the consequences of their actions." She jabbed her finger toward the open industrial door, through which they could see the globe of Petipa like a giant red ornament hanging off the steel tree of the space elevator. "We've been lied to our whole lives. Now, we have the opportunity to do the right thing, but we can't do it if we keep fighting amongst ourselves."

The other farmers drifted into the storage room, surely attracted by their raised voices. Fritz clenched his fists by his side, his face burning. He met the gaze of each of them in turn. Was it rage or shame that flushed his cheeks?

"Are we doing this re-sorting thing or not?" someone asked.

Klara kept her eyes glued to Fritz. "I don't know," she said. "Are we?"

Fritz ran a hand through his messy hair and then clapped twice, which made the nutcrackers freeze their motion.

"Well, don't just stand there," he said to the other farmers after a moment. "Grab a bag and let's get sorting."

Uncle and Nephew

They labored through the day, explaining the situation to each farmer who arrived later with their bag of recalled Pirlipat nuts. The faceless nutcrackers sorted out dozens of the bad nuts—*no*, Klara corrected herself, *the sacred nuts*. Their mutation served an important purpose, and it would serve that purpose again, once Dross worked his magic. He had left the factory hours ago, having first performed some tune-ups on the nutcracker androids and the other machines. *Better for him to get cracking on the harder nut*, Klara thought, *while the rest of us handle this.*

Since the nutcrackers needed no rest, the humans coordinated shifts to keep the conveyor belts full through the night as well. Klara worked until her hands ached so badly that she could hardly grip the ration bags. Normally, this would be done in smaller batches, and loaded into the machines directly from the tree shakers that gathered the nuts from the orchard floor.

"Where's Plum?" she asked one of the other farmers. Fritz, of course, had taken his leave early and was nowhere to be seen.

No one had seen the fairy in at least an hour, except for one of Ginger's children, who babbled something about a giant white bird. Ginger told the child to shoosh, but Klara understood. Plum must have flown home to Candy Mountain. Maybe she'd never intended to stay, as Klara assumed.

She did one last round to check that the conveyors and packaging assembly lines were working smoothly, and then paused, watching the nutcrackers' mechanical, repetitive movements. She'd never before considered them more than part of the factory's machinery, but Nathan certainly was. This harvest needed to be sorted as quickly as possible, but should she offer the nutcrackers a break? Was it only her own weariness projecting, or did even the conveyors creak and whine as though they were tired and strained?

Klara bit her lip and watched for a moment longer. The humans groaned as they lifted and paused to rub their hands or lower backs, but the nutcrackers never faltered, adjusting only to respond to the work in front of them.

They were fine. It would be fine. Klara went back to Silber House to shower and crash for the night.

The house was still a mess from the party, but cleaning up would have to wait until later. As soon as she awoke the next morning, Klara was back at the factory. No other humans were there, and to her dismay, the nutcrackers stood still as statues next to the empty, moving conveyor belt.

"Oh no," Klara groaned. She'd overworked them after all.

Klara snapped her fingers in front of the face of the closest one. Or rather, the smooth casing where a face should be. The nutcracker's head swiveled toward her.

"Awaiting orders, Ms. Silber," the nutcracker said. The voice was stilted, robotic, not at all the smooth and natural flow with which Nathan spoke.

"Are you in distress?" she asked.

"No, Ms. Silber," the nutcracker responded. "All of my systems are functional and up to date."

"I see," she said. "Are you able to continue?"

"Awaiting orders."

"Repeat yesterday's objective."

"Unable to comply. Product not present."

"Give me a second."

Klara hauled two ration bags from the storage room and emptied them onto the conveyor. The nutcrackers sprang back to life, plucking out the corrupted nuts and tossing them into a barrel, letting the rest fall through into the machine that would repackage them for transport. Several whole barrels were ready to go, but half the original harvest still waited in the storage room.

While the nutcrackers sorted at least that small batch, Klara followed an odd sound until she discovered Dross on the second floor. He worked furiously at a complicated equation on the whiteboard in her parents' old office.

"Good morning!" Klara chirped, trying to imbue as much cheer into her voice as possible.

Dross jumped at her greeting and fumbled his marker. It rolled underneath the desk. With a groan, he sank to his creaking knees and reached underneath to fish it out.

Klara dropped down and retrieved it for him in a single swipe. She held the marker out. He took it back, but then had to plunk it onto the desk so he could use both hands to pull himself back to standing. Klara stopped the marker from rolling onto the floor again.

"If I'd known you were here, I'd have brought you some tea," she said.

"No need, no need." He gestured distractedly toward a cold electric kettle on the far end of the desk.

"The others will be back any minute now." Klara hoped she could manifest it to be true. "Wouldn't you be more comfortable in your own workshop?"

Dross shook his head. "The workshop is dreadfully cold this time of year."

Klara raised an eyebrow. The factory had big open doors to let out the dust and particles from the nut processing, and though there was one geothermal pipe that ran through these upper administrative rooms, it was hardly any warmer here than it would be working outside.

"Okay," Dross admitted. "It was the thumping I couldn't take."

"Thumping?"

"The rustling, murmuring, and constant throbbing from behind the locked pantry door," he clarified. Louise, trapped in Dross's kitchen, must have been trying to claw her way out. "The machines here are noisy too, but it's a constant white noise that I can block out. The irregular thumping was hugely distracting."

"You've had a breakthrough, then?" Klara asked.

"Not quite. But I have learned some things."

She was about to offer encouragement, laced with urgency, when a different voice rang through the noise of the machines, calling up to her from downstairs like a hundred bright trumpets blowing cheerfully.

"Klara?"

Her heart leapt, never before so happy to hear her own name. She left Dross to his madness and hurried out of the office.

"Nathan!" Klara took the steps three at a time to meet him on the factory floor. She raced up and planted a kiss right on his metallic lips. He barked out a surprised laugh, and if androids were capable of blushing, he certainly would have.

Klara stepped back from him and suddenly registered his companions: not only Plum, but a whole group of fairies, clustered nervously outside the factory.

Klara looked a question at him, and fortunately he was just as good at interpreting human expressions as he was the fairies' dances.

"Plum reported back that you had rallied all the humans to work together."

"Not *all*, perhaps," Klara said, despair creeping in at the lack of help that arrived this morning. But even as she said it, she heard the whir of an electric tractor pulling up the driveway, and saw the plume of dust from another approaching on the road.

"She tried to do the same, but the clan leaders forbade it. These—" Nathan swept a hand toward the nervous fairies. "—are the clanless generation. The ones who were never able to take part in the transformation ritual. They're here to help. *We're* here to help."

Klara could kiss him again. She settled for a quick cheer instead, two fists punching the air and a little hop.

"How do you say 'thank you' in their language?" she asked.

Nathan showed her a quick and easy rock step, and Klara approached the group of fairies, repeating it. The fairies tittered and bowed, grinning at her with their razor sharp teeth.

The other humans wearily drifted in, working together with the fairies to load the remaining ration bags onto the machines. Nathan took his place next to the other nutcrackers.

"Are you sure you wouldn't rather do something else?" Klara asked him.

"Nonsense," he said with a broad grin. "I'm designed for this."

"Yes, but do you *want* to do the work of a nutcracker?"

Nathan's hands darted over the conveyor belt, sorting the nuts nearly twice as fast as his colleagues. He rocked his head from side to side as if considering Klara's question. "I wouldn't want to do *only* this," he said after a moment. "But I'm capable of the work and I enjoy it."

"That's more than I can say for most of us," Klara admitted.

Ginger and Pranab struggled with a large sack, and Klara left Nathan to rush over and lift the back end of it, barely preventing a spill that would have sent Pirlipat nuts rolling all over the factory floor.

Sometime mid-day, Dross wandered out of the upstairs office, muttering to himself. Klara set aside the broom she'd been using to sweep dust and broken shells from the factory floor, and called to Nathan. He turned one eye toward her and kept the other focused on the conveyor belt, in a way that reminded Klara uncannily of how Dross's cyborg eye sometimes moved separately from his organic one. She motioned with her head toward Dross, pacing along the upstairs railing in slow, steady steps. Nathan nodded sharply. He left off the sorting, and hit a button below the conveyor belt that slowed it down to a pace the other nutcrackers could better keep up with.

Klara linked her arm around Nathan's and guided him toward the staircase. Dross did a double take as he lifted his head to see Klara and Nathan coming up the stairs. His muttering trailed off.

"I don't believe you've been properly introduced," Klara said.

Dross met them at the top of the stairs and stood face-to-face with the nutcracker. His cyborg eye dilated and contracted; his lips parted in wonder. The resemblance in their features was unmistakable, Dross's years shaved away into Nathan's youthful face. They contemplated each other for a long moment—maker and machine, creator and creation. Finally, the nutcracker extended a hand and said, "Call me Nathan, please."

Dross looked down at the proffered hand for a second before he clasped his enthusiastically around it. "Extraordinary." His eyes danced over Nathan's face with the pride of an uncle reunited with a nephew who has grown and done great things since they last saw each other. "I can see the intelligence in your eyes, subtleties of emotion in your face that were not there before."

Then Dross glanced uncertainly at Klara. "The others?"

"Don't seem to be any more self-aware than our house vacuum," Klara said. "Whatever circuit Fritz tripped in Nathan, he must have avoided when he manipulated the others. Or else Nathan is such a superior specimen that it was only a matter of time before he awoke." She winked at him.

"Be that as it may," Nathan said, "I am feeling the urge to get back to work."

"Of course," Klara said. "Once this is done, we'll have all the time in the world to contemplate the miracle of your consciousness."

Dross watched Nathan descend the staircase and walk back to the machines. Klara stepped closer to the old man, dropping her voice. "Tell me why some of Nathan's programming is based on soldier droids."

Dross flushed. He nodded toward the office and Klara followed him in that direction.

"My goal has always been to make us obsolete," he said as they walked. "The debtors, I mean. Petipa will likely always be dependent on Eta, but if the work is more efficiently done by androids, they'll have little reason to keep importing human workers, and this whole indentured servitude can come to an end."

"That explains the nutcrackers, but not the soldier part."

They'd reached the office by now, and Dross sat on the edge of the paper-strewn desk, staring at the floor. His cyborg eye rolled over toward her.

"They may not care. Even if androids were more efficient, they may prefer to keep indenturing humans. There are some who believe those who serve on Eta are better prepared for the building of Petipa."

"The... building?" Klara shook her head, reality crashing in on her yet again. "The Colony is still being built?"

"It was to be a work in progress for at least a hundred years, or so they said when we first arrived," Dross confirmed.

So Klara's parents had only traded in their garden spade for a masonry trowel. It wasn't at all the utopic retirement she'd been picturing her whole life. She rolled that idea around in her head, reconsidered everything she thought she'd known against everything she knew now.

"But the nutcracker soldier?" Klara prompted, trying to stay focused on the question she'd asked.

"Petipa is rife with worker uprisings and political disputes. I didn't want to get involved, but I thought if they didn't care about the androids as a replacement for agricultural workers, perhaps the Petipa government would be interested in a stronger weapon."

"Interested enough to grant your invitation," Klara said flatly.

"Yes," Dross admitted. "Though with my history, I doubt they'll grant it to me no matter what. At this point, I'm not sure I even want the invitation. It should be the young who are offered the opportunity. There's nothing there for me. Plus, well, I like it here." He sounded embarrassed.

"Is life on Petipa actually any better than here?" Klara mused after a moment. Dross only shrugged.

Klara glanced at his cryptic formulations on the whiteboard. If the space elevator were destroyed, she'd never have the chance to find out.

"I've distracted you long enough," she said abruptly, and fled back to the factory floor where she could blame the tears that stung her eyes on the dust and debris in the air.

⸺◆⸺

At some point during the long day, Dross clambered down the steps and rushed across the factory floor like a whirlwind. He skidded to a stop, doubled back, and grabbed a handful of the sacred nuts out of the barrel. Those, he tossed into a beaker he carried, and then he darted off before Klara could ask him what was going on.

She shrugged at the others and said, "Breakthrough?" letting herself hope it was true.

Over the course of the day, Klara learned a few more of the fairies' dance-words, and began to recognize several others.

With the last of the ration bags emptied onto the conveyor belt, Klara brought out the leftover nog and cider and whatever non-nut-based pastries hadn't been tossed on the floor during the party. Some of the farmers took off right away, but others stuck around to celebrate. Even Nathan held a mug, even though he couldn't imbibe the drink—to feel like part of the group, he said.

"One problem solved." Klara looked into her cup. "But we're not in the clear yet." She downed her cider, and then recruited Nathan and a few of the older nutcrackers to help her roll the barrels over to the incinerator. Before they dumped the last one, she grabbed a handful and stowed them in the pockets of her work pants.

"What are you taking those for?" Nathan asked.

"Dross grabbed some earlier," she said. "He might need another sample when he comes back. That's assuming, of course, that he needed them for scientific purposes, and that he hasn't gone mad and decided he'd rather live out the rest of his days as a giant rat."

"A highly unlikely scenario," Nathan said with a chuckle.

"I've been thinking," Klara said as they wandered back toward the celebration, "how we can let others know the fairies' story."

"Others?" Nathan asked. "You mean the humans on Petipa?"

"Yes, or even Earth, if we can manage a transmission. This isn't a history that should remain hidden. If it was widely known what was done to them, it would change how everyone views the Colony. Dross says the workers on Petipa are unsatisfied with their conditions. Perhaps a revelation like this could destabilize the government enough to let them make real change."

Nathan frowned, and Klara recognized that a being built from the template of a soldier probably wasn't capable of viewing a phrase like "destabilize the government" in a positive light. She might have felt the same herself only a few days before.

"When there's corruption," she tried, "it must be sorted out, yes? And how can you recognize a bad nut if you don't have all the information about what makes it bad?"

"I think I see your aim. So how do you propose to approach such a controversial reveal?"

"Through spectacle!" Klara took his hand and used him to steady herself as she leaped in place with pointed toes, in an approximation of what the fairies did when they were trying to get someone's attention. Attention, she got; the fairies and the farmers who remained in the factory paused their conversations and turned their eyes toward Klara. "We can let the fairies tell their story in their own way, but add in a narrative element that humans can easily understand."

"You want to put on a performance?" Nathan asked.

"Together, yes, we'll create a play, a musical drama. A sweet fiction that exposes an acid truth. Sugar softens the taste of even the most bitter nuts."

Some of the farmers rolled their eyes, but others nodded thoughtfully. Ginger's children were already chattering about what type of role they each could play.

Klara took one of Nathan's hands in both of hers. "Won't you ask them if they'll do it?"

Nathan found a clear space on the factory floor, and danced the proposal.

The Kingdom of Dolls

Now there *was* a reason to clean up the solarium. Klara swept and shoved furniture to the side and puzzled over how she could repurpose some of the Christmas-themed decorations for the show. They had two days until the ship from Petipa docked at the top of the space elevator, and Klara must have this performance done and recorded by then so she could hand deliver a hard copy to the ship captain. She threw herself into planning and rehearsals, assisted by Nathan's translations, while both humans and fairies came and went from what felt like an extension of the truncated Winter Party.

Dross arrived, accompanied by Fritz, for some reason, but they didn't stay, and Klara didn't realize Plum and Nathan had gone with them until all four arrived back at Silber House later that evening. She managed fine without Nathan's interpretative skills, gaining more and more ground in the language of movement now that they shared a goal.

Klara was working on a sequence with Ginger's children depicting the farmers' arrival on Eta when the front door swung open. Dross, Nathan, Fritz, and Plum bustled in with a gust of cold wind. Plum shook snowflakes from her wings. Nathan stomped clumps of snow from his boots onto the already muddy foyer tiles. Fritz smiled at Klara, and that's how she knew something very strange must have happened.

"We did it!" Dross announced. Plum twirled in a celebratory motion.

"What is it you've done?" Klara asked.

"I *told* you my orchard produced fewer of the bad nuts," Fritz boasted.

"His plot sits on a mineral deposit," Dross explained, and Klara snapped her mouth shut to trap the snarky response that almost escaped. "The mineral neutralizes the introduced fungus that has gripped the roots of so many other trees. There is much work to be done to reverse the damage to the Pirlipat tree, but the fairies were sufficiently impressed by my designs that they gave us a sample of the antidote that will treat anyone currently transformed."

"Are you sure it works?" Klara asked. She strode toward the door, not sure why they had left it open to allow so much cold air in.

"It works," another voice said from outside. Klara paused with the door part way open and gasped. Louise stepped out of the shadows. She looked thin and haggard, aged ten years in ten days, but she was alive, and she was human. Klara flung the door wide—who cared about cold air when there were dear friends to be hugged—and threw her arms around Louise.

Klara released the hug and held up a finger, then rushed to the coat closet. Many of the coats left from the party had been reutilized as costumes by now, but she easily located the coat Louise wore to the party and held it out to her.

Louise laughed as she accepted the coat. The bright yellow and faux fur contrasted comically with the oversized brown pants she'd borrowed from Dross. But as soon as Louise wrapped the coat around herself, her expression darkened.

"I don't entirely remember what happened," she said. "But Dross explained some of it to me. Klara, I'm so sorry."

Klara shut the door and waved her apology away. "Not your fault, not at all. If anyone should be sorry, it's Fritz." She shot him a glare.

He nodded solemnly. "I am," he said.

Klara blinked at him in surprise.

Fritz shrugged. "I told you, if I'd known what the bad nuts did to people, I'd have never messed with the nutcrackers."

"If I'd understood your concerns about our system, you might never have felt compelled to do it in the first place," Klara admitted. She extended a hand, if not exactly in friendship, then at least in solidarity. "Truce?"

He shook her hand, one quick sharp pump. Well, that was certainly a step in the right direction.

"Come on," she said to Louise. "Let's get you some food that won't have you growing fur and fangs."

Klara settled Louise in the solarium with a bowl of hot food. Leaving her to watch the rehearsal, she whispered to Dross, "What of the others? Ginger's husband Benjamin, for example. There are seven people missing; if they were likewise affected by the corrupted nuts, then distributing the antidote presents a whole other challenge."

"It is already done." Dross motioned expansively toward the window, where the space elevator was barely visible through the snowstorm that wrapped itself around the valley.

Klara thought at first that he meant something to do with the space elevator, but then she understood. "The snow?"

"Indeed," Dross said. "Cloud seeding. The antidote won't harm anyone who's unaffected, and it should do the trick for anyone wandering the woods thinking they're a giant rat."

"Should?" Klara asked.

Just then, a tentative tap came at the back door, so light that they almost didn't hear it. Klara passed through the kitchen and cracked the door open. A man stood shivering outside the mudroom, his clothes torn and tattered, a bewildered expression on his face.

"Klara Silber?" He squinted up at her from a few steps down. "Sorry, I... I don't quite know how I found myself here."

"Benjamin." Klara grinned. "Come in, please. Ginger's been looking for you."

A glass shattered on the floor and Klara spun toward the sound to see Ginger staring wide-eyed at her husband as if she'd seen a ghost. The spell broke with a shriek of joy that Klara thought might shatter even more glasses. She got out of the way just in time as Ginger raced across the kitchen and threw her arms around Benjamin. Her children, attracted by their mother's shriek, flooded into the kitchen and swarmed him too.

After they managed to pry the children off their father's legs, Klara put them back to work finalizing their scene in the performance, while Ginger took Benjamin home to get him cleaned up and cared for.

Several others, Klara learned later, also found their way home in the snowstorm that night. None had any memory of where they'd been. Six of the missing seven, restored and returned.

Once dark fully settled in, Silber House emptied out, leaving only Klara, Nathan, Dross, and Plum. Dross turned Klara's window into a whiteboard, marking equations across her Christmas tree outline as he worked through the final problems of how much of the mineral to apply to the orchards. It would take an entire growing season, he explained, to know for sure if the sacred nuts had been returned to their former potency.

Klara snuggled up next to Nathan, watching the recording of the performance she'd spent the last couple of days putting together.

"What do you think?" she asked once the video finished.

"Riveting, entertaining," he said. "A sure five stars."

If she could pinch his metal skin, she would have.

"Truly," she implored.

"Truly," he said. "It's a story worth telling, and though you lacked the resources for a large cinematic production, I am confident it will still capture the imagination of those who watch it."

"Can it be sent to Earth?" Klara directed the question to Dross, who continued to mutter to himself something about balancing nitrogen and phosphorus cycles with the local mineral. "Dross?" He startled and looked over at her. "My recording. Can it be sent to Earth? Before we deliver it to Petipa? That way, even if Petipa suppresses it, they won't be able to intercept the transmission to Earth, so the truth will be heard, at least by some."

"That's it!" He turned back to his window equations, scrubbing out a graph with the sleeve of his shirt and scribbling something new in its place. "Yes, yes," he said to Klara with a distracted glance over his shoulder. "First thing in the morning, I'll help you send it."

Klara set the screen on the table and snuggled closer into the crook of Nathan's arm. He was so warm that she sometimes forgot he was actually a machine, and he seemed more human by the day. Plum stretched out on the rug, head resting on her folded arms, wings draping over her body like a blanket. There were still problems to be solved, but for the first time since her parents left for Petipa, Klara fell asleep without a care in the world.

The Capital

Standing at the base, the space elevator truly did resemble a steel tree, the beams stretching out across the sky like a canopy. A light blinked to indicate the ship had docked at the top and was ready to receive the winter harvest. Klara pulled one of the corrupted Pirlipat nuts out of the pocket of her atmosphere suit and rolled it between her fingers, inspecting the whorled shell. Plum chirped a flute-like melody, which Klara didn't understand. Just like Klara, the fairy wore a thick protective suit, but in addition to protecting against the cold and maintaining oxygen as they climbed above the atmosphere in this cargo lift, Plum's would also serve to hide her wings.

"I must advise against this plan of yours," Nathan said.

"I know you must." She held a hand out and he squeezed her fingers affectionately. She stepped onto the elevator platform along with the winter harvest.

"Are you sure you don't want me to come with you?" Nathan asked.

"I do," Klara said. "But introducing both a fairy and a sentient android at the same time might be a bit too much." Really, with his soldier programming, Klara feared that they would commandeer him and end up turning him against the farmers. But she wouldn't speak such horrible thoughts to his face. And what she'd said was true enough: she needed Petipa focused on the issue of the fairies.

Klara and Plum rode with the harvest all the way to the top. Eta shrank below them, becoming a curved dome against a starry background.

The worker who opened the airlock jumped when he saw the two of them. "Oh, sorry, you startled me," he said. "I was under the impression that there had been no invitations issued this quarter."

"I need to see the captain." Klara's voice was muffled and small through the suit's speaker.

"Sorry?"

"The captain. I need to see them immediately."

"I don't know if that's..." The worker trailed off as his gaze went to two of the workers who were struggling to unload the harvest shipment.

"They've got it locked down," one of them said, pointing to a digital padlock.

"Let me talk to the captain, or else you don't get this shipment." Klara held his gaze, trying to keep her voice steady. Plum shifted nervously behind Klara, bouncing foot to foot.

"Are you striking?"

Klara held her ground. "That depends on you."

The worker stabbed a finger toward Klara. "The government *will* hear about this."

"I hope they do," she said. "We have quite a lot to tell them about."

He whispered something into a radio on his shoulder, then flung his arm toward the doorway. "Come on, then."

Klara swallowed thickly as they crossed the bridge from the loading dock onto the ship. She'd imagined this moment so many times, but never like this. What she was about to do may well guarantee she'd never cross this bridge in good faith.

Klara took her helmet off as soon as they were inside, but Plum kept hers on. The dock worker led them through a narrow hallway. The walls were decorated with photographs of Petipa, showing all kinds of people, happy. *It's propaganda*, Klara told herself, but the smiling faces filled her with deep regret that she may never join them.

A door whooshed open, and Klara had to turn her eyes away from the photographs and back to the task at hand.

"Sir," the dock worker announced to a tall silver-haired woman. "The farmers of Eta who demanded an audience with you."

She rose, stiff and straight, reminding her of the way Nathan sometimes did when he was on guard. A much older round-faced man next to her did the same.

"I'm Captain Trutchen," the woman said, and didn't ask for Klara or Plum's names. "The Ensign tells me you're holding the harvest hostage. What is the meaning of this?"

Klara dropped the serious demeanor she'd taken with the dock worker and smiled widely at the two of them. "It is a true pleasure to meet you, Captain. I'm Klara Silber. I believe you met my parents last winter. We request that you deliver this important message to the highest levels of the Petipa government."

Klara held out the data stick she'd brought, featuring the recording she'd done with the fairies and the other farmers. It suddenly seemed silly, the little dance performance they'd put together, but she stuck to the plan.

Captain Trutchen stared at the data stick like Klara was trying to hand her a live snake. "Are you striking?"

That question again. Perhaps the farmers had more power for negotiation than they realized.

"No, no, nothing like that," Klara assured her. "We wouldn't endanger the lives of innocent people by withholding our shipment. But we do have information we need disseminated."

She lifted the data stick again, and this time Captain Trutchen swiped it away from her. Plum reached for her helmet, but Klara raised a hand to signal her to wait.

She'd just noticed the name stitched into the man's uniform: W. Confectioner. He did not look so old as Dross, but close. Perhaps his relative youth was simply that he hadn't lived a life of hard outdoor work as Dross and the other farmers of Eta had.

Everything Klara had practiced and envisioned for this encounter fled from her mind. This was Wendell Confectioner, Dross's old flame. The man who introduced the corruption to the Pirlipat nut and forced the fairies into hiding. Her gaze flickered to Captain Trutchen. Despite the captain's silver hair, the dark skin of her face was unlined, placing her at least a couple of decades younger than him. Did she know what he'd done?

Klara took one of the Pirlipat nuts from her pocket, and instead of handing it to the captain, like she'd planned, she cracked the shell with her teeth.

Smiling at Confectioner, she held out the shelled kernel in the palm of her hand. "We had a particularly good harvest this year. Won't you join me for a celebratory sample?"

Suspicion flickered across his face. "You think these kinds of gestures will shorten your debt?" He spat the last word like a curse.

"Sergeant," Captain Trutchen said sharply. "We don't want to show disrespect by refusing food from our friends. It's all they have, and it's very generous of them to share what they might have kept for themselves."

Sufficiently cowed, he plucked the kernel from Klara's hand and bit into it. Klara swallowed dryly, and though she hadn't eaten the nut, it felt like several sharp pieces were lodged in her throat. She wished she knew exactly how long it would be before the mutation took effect. Feeding the corrupted nut to someone hadn't been part of the plan, not at all. She'd meant only to deliver a sample of the mutation as proof, along with the data stick that told the story. But the presence of Wendell Confectioner necessitated a stronger response.

"Is that all?" Captain Trutchen asked, irritation thick in her voice. "We have a very tight schedule to meet our landing point on Petipa."

"No, I'm afraid that isn't all, Captain. You see, my companion here—" She brought Plum around in front but her next words were cut off when Confectioner doubled over.

"Confectioner, what's wrong?" Captain Trutchen put a hand on his arm and then flinched away as fur sprouted through his uniform sleeve. Captain Trutchen called for medical officers. *Perfect*, Klara thought. They needed witnesses. If enough people saw, if more people knew, then it would be harder to cover up.

Captain Trutchen grabbed Confectioner under the arms and hauled him into a chair.

"What have you done?" she demanded of Klara. "What was in that nut?"

"This—" Klara pointed to Sergeant Confectioner, whose face stretched into a snout, becoming more rodent-like by the second. "—is what was done to her kind." She pointed toward Plum, who removed her helmet and peeled the suit down to her waist. She flared her wings dramatically.

Captain Trutchen's professional demeanor cracked, and the surprise on her face told Klara she hadn't known.

"These people lived on Eta before us, and were nearly wiped out so we could use it for our agricultural purposes. Sergeant Confectioner himself engineered the fungus that causes this transformation he now suffers."

His uniform was being shredded by his morphing body, and a long gray tail sprouted, whipping wildly back and forth. He held his head in his paws, clearly still consumed by the agony of the transformation, not ready to direct that anguish outward in an attack just yet. Klara needed to act quickly if she was going to avoid becoming a casualty to her own spontaneous revenge.

She held up a bottle conspicuously labeled *Antidote*. Captain Trutchen swiped at it and Klara made it disappear with a sleight of hand Dross taught her many years ago.

"Give it to him," Captain Trutchen ordered. "Fix this; reverse what you caused."

"What *he* caused," Klara corrected. "The fairies needed something from us before they'd share this antidote. I need something from you before I'll do the same."

The doors opened and two medical officers rushed in, balking at the sight of the transformed officer. He lunged out of the chair toward them and they recovered from their shock quickly enough to get his paws behind his back. Yellow teeth snapped at the air.

"What do you want, Miss Silber?" Captain Trutchen asked. "What are your terms?"

Ah, I have a name again, Klara thought bitterly.

She drew in a deep breath to embolden herself. "We want the truth to be publicly acknowledged by the government of Petipa, and reparations to be made to the indigenous beings of Eta. Further, we want an end to the indentured servitude program."

"Without the program, no one will stay on Eta to do the work. Petipa will starve."

"Some will stay," Klara said.

"Why would they? There's nothing there."

"There's plenty there," Klara said. "There's the songs we sing to pass the time in the Pirlipat orchards. There's the reflection of the sunset in the glass of Candy Mountain. There's the warmth of a geothermal floor after a day in cold boots. There's the surprise of everyone's newest dress at the Winter Party, and the fresh wines we ferment just for ourselves every summer. We may not be a colony, but we're something better. We're a community."

Klara surprised herself with the heartfelt speech. A few days ago, she would have jumped at any chance to change her fate and board the ship to Petipa.

"That's all lovely and poetic," the captain said sarcastically, "but I can't wave a magic wand and make all your demands come true. And if you think I'll throw you in the brig for this stunt and give you a free ride to Petipa, you're sorely mistaken."

Sergeant Confectioner was still transforming, nearly all rat by now. One of the medical officers wrestled him down to the floor and held a knee to his back to keep him down. The other called for backup.

Klara approached slowly and uncorked the antidote. It could be absorbed through the skin, as with the snow, so she splashed the liquid onto Confectioner's fur. Almost instantly, the transformation ceased and began to reverse. Klara tossed the other Pirlipat nut she'd brought to Captain Trutchen, who caught it with fumbling surprise.

Klara pointed to the Sergeant, then to Plum. "He corrupted a sacred tree and turned her people into mindless, violent monsters, so they'd kill each other and leave the planet vacant for us. Do what you think is right," Klara said. "The spring harvest will be ready on time if you do."

One Year Later

Klara tapped her foot on the warm tile floor of the foyer, nervously watching the door.

"No one's going to come," she said. After the disaster of last year's Winter Party, why would they?

Nathan stepped down from a ladder, the last tinsel streamers hung. "They'll come. It's early, yet."

But despite his reassurance, Klara kept flitting around, fretting, picking at the beads on her new green dress. Klara had taken a potted coniferous tree from the tree nursery and brought it inside in front of the big window, blocking the view of the space elevator. A proper Christmas tree, decorated with lights and tinsel and colorful glass bulbs. A real tree looked better than a steel tree, anyway.

Despite her worries, Nathan was right. They all came: The neighbors from the nearest farms, and from the ones a hundred miles away. Louise and Alicia arrived together arm in arm. Pranab had the most elaborate kurta, as usual, decorated with delicate shining stones he'd collected on his fairy-assisted trek up Candy Mountain. Ginger and Benjamin arrived with their whole family, including a newborn in an embroidered red and green sling.

The fairies entered nearly all together, flitting into Klara's solarium with the buzz of an insect swarm. Three of the clans had moved down to reclaim the fertile valley, and negotiations had been made to permit the continuation of farming without disturbing the fairies' traditional nesting sites, where they bent trees and bushes into elaborate canopies, shaping the forest to their needs in beautiful and almost invisible ways. The Inks chose to stay in Candy Mountain, still distrustful of the humans.

The fairies even helped make this the most productive growing season in Eta's history. A plant the humans had tagged as a noxious weed could actually be mulched into a highly effective fertilizer, and the fairies demonstrated an easy way to recycle runoff water rather than let it pollute the river. The fairies adored the summer squashes and fragrant herbs the humans had brought from Earth, and they borrowed tools and 3D printers—often without asking—to make their nesting process easier. Conflicts and misunderstandings took place, of course, but the humans and the fairies found ways to make their cohabitation beneficial for both groups.

Klara watched the two species dance together now in the center of the solarium: the fairies stood in a line, pointed their toes toward the center and bowed, and a row of humans repeated the gesture. Then they paired up, walked around their partner in a circle and switched, creating an intricate, spinning design that was a dance as well as a song, a conversation as well as an entertainment.

Fritz came up beside her, arms crossed.

"Congratulations." The bitterness infused into the word meant he probably wasn't congratulating her on a successful Winter Party.

She frowned. "What do you mean?"

"The message from Petipa? Don't act like you haven't seen it."

"I haven't!" She'd been far too busy with the harvest and party preparations to check messages. She rushed to the kitchen now and tapped the screen, skimming until she found what Fritz must have seen.

There, under the usually blank list of passengers to be picked up was a single name: *Klara Silber, debt forgiven, paid by information.*

She blinked at the screen for a few moments. It was all she'd ever wanted, to ascend the steel tree and ride a spaceship to Petipa, to her true destiny. Except, she could no longer see herself in that future. To leave behind everything they'd built here, to leave and abandon Louise and Dross and Nathan... Dross said this was his home now, and Klara found that she felt the same. She had no desire to ditch it and venture into the unknown chaos of Petipa Colony.

The demand she'd made of Captain Trutchen for an end of indentured servitude was still under review, but new ships from Earth had been stalled, and those currently en route were being given the choice to join Eta or Petipa, with full understanding of the hardships of each. There had been far more transparency in the communications between Eta and Petipa over the past year, enough that the farmers unanimously agreed not to withhold shipments as Klara had threatened.

Politics were shifting, and more people were becoming sympathetic to their situation. Wendell Confectioner had been stripped of his position and power, and scientists were back to working on the problem of making Petipa more self-sufficient and less reliant on harvests from Eta. It would be a long process, but Klara was confident that with the right pressures, they'd eventually change the trajectory.

Klara thought for a moment longer, and her resolve grew. She sent back a message: *Invitation appreciated but declined. Recommend change of passenger: Fritz Huzar, debt paid through hard work, cooperation, and innovation.*

The "cooperation" part was perhaps a stretch, though he'd shown the capacity for it once or twice.

Recommendation pending, came an automatic reply.

Klara closed the screen. She considered telling Fritz what she'd done, but he'd know soon enough if the change was approved. He could stay mad at her for the duration of the party. It was tradition, by now.

When the moment felt right, Klara clanged a glass to get everyone's attention. She stood beside the tree, paused for dramatic effect, then nodded to Nathan, who tapped the control panel on the wall. Electricity rushed in and the tree lit up with white and purple lights. Everyone oohed and awed appropriately. Klara admired her own handiwork. Of course, she hadn't done it all herself. Nathan had helped decorate, along with Ginger's two oldest children—happy for the distraction while Ginger was preoccupied with her newest little one. But just as Klara opened her mouth to give credit to her helpers, the overhead lights flashed, and a steady drumbeat pulled everyone's attention toward the foyer.

Klara accepted Nathan's hand and steadied herself as she hopped off the platform. She tucked her arm into his elbow crook.

"He always has to show me up, doesn't he?" she said, but couldn't help a smile from sneaking onto her lips.

A line of nutcrackers marched into the solarium, drums fastened over the shoulders of the front two. Dross had told her the newest generation of nutcrackers were ready, but this was the first she'd seen them. Their faces looked different from Nathan's, which was a relief. None of them had gained sentience, Dross assured her, and likely wouldn't unless something unusual happened. Klara remained skeptical about that—Nathan had awoken, so the possibility lay dormant in all of them. Perhaps they *should* awaken, be able to make decisions for themselves rather than be locked into the work humans made them for.

The crowd parted to make room for the procession of nutcracker soldiers, who lined up in front of Klara's tree. Dross followed them, wearing that same awful yellow frock coat he always did.

"The newest generation of nutcrackers will assist at the Silber House processing plant during busy harvest times," Dross announced. "But during the rest of the year, they will be available to assist every farm and orchard, according to whatever is needed."

Klara had insisted on that new policy, and she watched everyone's faces, pleased at the joy the pronouncement sparked on some of them. Fritz still crossed his arms and sulked, but he softened a bit when Klara winked at him.

Then Dross turned his attention to the fairies, and called Plum up to the front.

"This is a special winter harvest, a monumental one." With a dramatic sleight of hand, he produced a large yellow nut and presented it to Plum with a bow. The sorting had been far easier this year, with the sacred nut returned to what it was supposed to look like. At least, Klara hoped this was what it was supposed to look like. Plum tentatively accepted it from Dross, holding the shell up to the light to inspect.

A cold breeze rushed through the solarium, and everyone turned toward the foyer. The leader of the Inks clan, wings fully extended, strode into the solarium. The rest of her clan trailed behind, and the other fairies danced a greeting and a plea for peace. The tension in the room ratcheted up several degrees. Every muscle in Klara's shoulders and neck tightened. If Dross's solution for the Pirlipat nuts wasn't accurate, then the Inks' threat from a year ago would come to fruition. The space elevator would still be destroyed. Plum confirmed months ago that the Inks clan was stockpiling combustible minerals, and planned to go through with the destruction unless a reversal of the corruption was proven.

Partially to stop the cold air, and partially to keep her own body from combusting with fear, Klara rushed over to shut the front door behind them. By the time she got back to the solarium, the Inks had lined up opposite of the nutcrackers, and Dross had resumed his speech.

"As you may be aware," Dross said. "Plum and the others of her generation were never able to undergo an important coming-of-age ritual and join a clan according to their customs. That can change this very night."

Plum cracked the shell easily with her sharp teeth and split the kernel in half. She motioned to another young fairy, who stepped forward to accept the proffered half. The two of them performed an intricate handshake, like a children's clapping game, and then they each consumed their half of the nut. Hand in hand, they glided to the center of the room in a beautiful slow ballet, and then settled into meditative cross-legged seats, back-to-back.

Dross gave a silent order to the new nutcracker androids. They marched forward to encircle the two fairies, ready to act as a shield if something went awry. The Inks leader stepped forward in alarm, but the others repeated the dance for peace and she retreated. The nutcrackers kneeled so the crowd could see over their heads. Klara wished she could clasp Nathan's hand, but he was there in the circle with his mechanical brothers. He lifted his head slightly and gave her a wink, surely an attempt at reassurance. The nutcrackers would protect the partygoers from a repeat of last year's disaster, but if this transformation didn't go according to tradition, they could be in store for a much larger disaster.

Plum began to transform first, doubling forward as her shoulders grew and her face contorted. Klara could hardly breath as she watched Plum's mouth and nose elongate into a toothy snout, her hands curl into sharp claws. It was no different so far from what she'd observed happen to Wendell Confectioner on board the ship last year.

The fairies emitted little high-pitched squeaks, and though Klara knew much of their language by now, she had no idea what those sounds meant. The nutcrackers held steady.

Then the transformation stopped halfway, not fully rat the way Louise and the others had been. Plum retained her wings, and brown fur sprouted from her arms, but not from the rest of her body. Her partner's transformation was similar, with a little less claw and a little more shoulder bulk. The two stood, and each took a long stride in opposite directions before pirouetting to come face to face. They circled each other for a long moment, and then began something that looked like half martial arts combat, half dance battle. Far different from the brutal, rage-filled attacks of the giant rats who had consumed the corrupted nuts.

"It's like capoeira," Klara whispered to Dross, remembering a video she'd once watched in the archives.

"Much like it," Dross agreed.

Plum appeared to win the battle, and representatives from two clans leaped straight over the nutcracker guards. One claimed Plum, the other claimed her partner with equal celebration. Their features transformed back to normal, though the bruises and scratches they'd earned in the battle remained. Nathan moved aside, and the Inks clan leader stepped forward to effortlessly elevate Plum into an overhead lift.

Klara rushed over to Nathan. "Is that good?"

"I believe so," he said. Nathan danced with one of the other Inks for a moment, and then announced to the whole room, "The sacred nuts have been restored!"

The whole room cheered, and two more of the fairy youth stepped into the ring.

The other nutcrackers remained on guard, but Nathan stayed with the spectators now. He leaned down to whisper in Klara's ear while they watched the second round. "It's not about who wins or loses, but what movements they choose during the battle that determines which clan they belong with. Plum chose the shorter route to victory, but with the more difficult moves."

Once the second match successfully concluded, Dross had the new nutcrackers bring in a whole crate of the sacred nuts, and everyone, human and fairy and android, watched the spectacle late into the night.

Everyone, that is, except for Klara and Nathan, who after the third match, sneaked out the back door and borrowed one of the giant swans who roosted in the orchard behind Silber House. While they snuggled together in the saddle, the swan rose above the treetops and soared over the fertile valley. Candy Mountain glowed in the moonlight, and the snow from a few nights before glittered across the fertile valley like sugar crystals. The swan soared over the untraversable lava lands, then swooped back around, dipping low over the treetops of the orchards. Not an ounce of regret panged her as the globe of Petipa shined through the clouds. Eta was home, and she found that thought brought only joy. Why should she covet a crowded alien city when there was such beauty around her?

"This truly is a wondrous place, isn't it?" Nathan said.

Klara smiled. "When you have the right eyes to see it."

About the Author

Photo by Halo Stone Photography

Sarena Ulibarri is a speculative fiction author and editor from the American Southwest. Her short stories have appeared in *Lightspeed*, *DreamForge*, *GigaNotoSaurus*, *Solarpunk Magazine*, and elsewhere, and nonfiction essays have appeared in *Strange Horizons* and *Grist*. Her novella, *Another Life*, was published by Stelliform Press in 2023. As an anthologist, she has curated and published several international volumes of optimistic climate fiction: *Glass and Gardens: Solarpunk Summers*

(2018), *Glass and Gardens: Solarpunk Winters* (2020), and *Multispecies Cities: Solarpunk Urban Futures* (2021).

Also by Sarena

Novellas
ANOTHER LIFE

Anthologies
SPECULATIVE STORY BITES
GLASS AND GARDENS: SOLARPUNK SUMMERS
GLASS AND GARDENS: SOLARPUNK WINTERS
MULTISPECIES CITIES: SOLARPUNK URBAN
FUTURES

www.ingramcontent.com/pod-product-compliance
Lightning Source LLC
Chambersburg PA
CBHW070515200726
48293CB00007B/2560